DANNY ORLIS
AND
RON'S CALL TO SERVICE

DANNY ORLIS

AND

RON'S CALL TO SERVICE

BERNARD PALMER

Please note that several books in the Danny Orlis series are published by Sword of the Lord Publications and are available for purchase on their website, www.swordbooks.com.

Danny Orlis and Ron's Call to Service
© 2024 by Bernard Palmer
All rights reserved. First edition 1963.
Second edition 2024.

Scripture quotations from The Authorized (King James) Version. Rights in the Authorized Version in the United Kingdom are vested in the Crown. Reproduced by permission of the Crown's patentee, Cambridge University Press.

Cover Artwork: Larry Lecheler
Editor: Charlene Miskimen

Aneko Press Youth

www.anekopress.com

Aneko Press, Life Sentence Publishing, and our logos are trademarks of Life Sentence Publishing, Inc.
203 E. Birch Street
P.O. Box 652
Abbotsford, WI 54405

JUVENILE FICTION / Religious / Christian / Action & Adventure
Paperback ISBN: 979-8-88936-006-3
eBook ISBN: 979-8-88936-007-0
10 9 8 7 6 5 4 3 2 1
Available where books are sold

CONTENTS

AUTHOR'S NOTE

Ron Orlis, who had been attending Cedarton Bible Institute, went to work for a construction company in northern Canada during the summer. The company liked his work so well that they offered him a substantial raise to stay with them. Having gotten a taste of what it was like to have a little money of his own and to be able to buy things, he decided to stay out of school and work for a year. However, it was obvious that he was outside the will of God.

Ron's twin sister, Roxie, was greatly concerned and wrote to him about it. When she got a check for a thousand dollars from him, she was especially disturbed because he had written that one reason he wanted to stay out of school and work was to make it easier for her while she was going to school.

Roxie became sick suddenly and very soon died of acute leukemia. Her death affected Ron deeply. When he went back to Cedarton Bible Institute to get her clothes, he found his uncashed check in her Bible, together with a note that said she planned to write him to see if it was all right to give the money to missions. Through these things Ron saw the sin of materialism that had crept into his life and kept him from Bible school that fall.

Chapel was going on and it was testimony time. Ron took this occasion to make a public confession of what had happened to him and to tell the whole school that he was going to quit his job and come back to CBI for the second semester.

His testimony, coupled with Roxie's death, touched off a revival on the campus. (You can read about these events in *The Orlis Twins and Roxie's Triumph*).

At this point we take up the adventures of the Orlis family once more.

CHAPTER 1

ROXIE'S GONE BUT NOT FORGOTTEN

Wind whipped across the Cedarton Bible Institute campus, driving snow in swirling eddies over frozen ground. Ron Orlis stood for a moment outside the chapel, facing into the wind. It stung his face and drove through his coat, but he scarcely noticed.

Ron had just given his testimony, admitting to the kids in chapel how Roxie's death had shaken him out of his materialism and lethargy for Christ. He had learned that life is fleeting, that even though he was young there was no assurance that he would live a long life. He realized that the most important thing in the world is to prepare for Christian service and serve the Lord now.

He stumbled down the chapel steps and blindly out to the road. Although he had come out to CBI expressly to get Roxie's clothes and books, he left them in the dormitory and started to walk to town. He couldn't go and get them. Not after what had just happened – what was happening, even now.

There was still an ache in Ron's heart, but it was different – more bearable. Indeed, a kind of joy shone through, and there was even a song in his soul.

Any number of people would have left the meeting and driven him to the Forester home where he was staying while he was in Cedarton, but he didn't want that. At the moment all he wanted was to be left alone.

Ron had not walked far when a car stopped beside him and the driver put down his window.

"I've got to go into town to catch a train, Ron. Hop in and I'll take you where you're going."

Ron turned slowly and stared at the man behind the wheel. It was almost as though he had not heard him.

"How about a ride?"

"Oh–oh, hello, Dr. Carter."

"Hop in, Ron. It's too cold to be walking today."

"Thanks anyway," he spoke hesitantly. "But I–I would just as soon walk. There are some things I've got to think out."

It was an hour or so later when Ron knocked at the Forester door where Danny Orlis had gone to wait for him.

"You should've called us," Mr. Forester began. "There wasn't any need for you to take a cab all the way in from the school."

Ron took off his coat and hung it in the hall closet. "I didn't take a cab. I walked." He crossed to the fireplace and for a time looked intently into the fire. "I had a chance to get a ride, but I turned it down."

His older brother, who was standing beside Harold Forester, nodded understandingly. For the space of a minute or so the only sound was that of the ticking of the clock. To Ron's tense nerves it seemed to thunder, though the sound was scarcely audible.

"I was about to ask Harold to take me out to CBI and see if I could help you with the packing. I thought the job might be bigger than you figured it would be."

Ron's eyes clouded. "The packing isn't going to take long. They have almost everything ready. I could have gotten it and been back a long time ago, Danny, but I just had to get away for a little while. I–I couldn't stand it anymore."

"I think I know just how you felt, Ron. If there's anything I can do, just let me know."

Mrs. Forester came to the living room door just then. "I just invited Danny and you to stay overnight, Ron. That would give you a little more time to go out and get Roxie's things. It–it might help to make it a little easier for you."

Ron glanced at his older brother. "It doesn't make much difference to me. What do you say, Danny? Can you stay, or do you have to get back this evening?"

"It doesn't make any difference whether I get back right away or not," he answered. "I told Kay and Dr.

Gordon at the mission that it might be several days before we get back. They're not expecting us right away."

Mrs. Forester took his reply as their decision to stay. "Then it's all settled. And I'm so glad that you're going to stay. We've been wanting to get a chance to visit with you. It seems so long since you and the–the others used to come over here so often."

She went back to the kitchen after a moment or two, and Harold Forester, sensing that Danny and Ron wanted to be alone, excused himself and went to his den. As soon as Mr. Forester was gone, Danny turned and looked at his younger brother.

"What happened at school today?" he asked quietly.

Ron's frown deepened. "What do you mean?"

"Something happened – to you, I mean. I can see it in your eyes. You're more at ease – more relaxed. You give the distinct impression of being almost happy."

Ron's chest expanded as he pulled in a deep breath and exhaled slowly. "Something did happen, Danny." A hush settled over his voice. "Something that should have happened a long time ago. I've just seen that I've been running away from the Lord."

Danny's gaze met his. "Have you, Ron?"

The younger boy's gaze did not waver. "You know that as well as I do." His voice broke and there was a brief interval before he could continue. "I used to think that I was so solid in my faith that nothing could sway me. But I found out that wasn't true, that any of us can drift away from God." His attention went back to the fire for a short space of time. "I've let materialism take over in my life. I wanted a car and clothes and spending money and all of the things that the average guy in the world would like to have. Before I realized it, I had let them crowd God out of my plans for the future. I even stayed out of Bible school this semester so I could get the things I wanted."

Danny nodded. "As a matter of fact, Kay and I have been very much concerned about you the past few months. We've been praying for you regularly."

"You tried to talk with me often enough, but I was too stupid to let you." Ron leaned back and crossed his legs. "You weren't the only ones who tried to talk with me. Roxie wrote to me about it several times. But I wouldn't listen to her, either. I kept using one excuse after another to stay out of school and on the job. I know now that Satan was just using those things to try and interfere with my following God's plan for my life."

Danny got to his feet and stood with his back to the fire. "Satan will do that every chance he gets."

"With the Lord's help that's all over for me, Danny." A new determination gripped Ron's voice. "I'm going back to school. I'm going to turn my life completely over to Him and let Him use me in any way He wishes."

Danny Orlis beamed. "That would make Roxie very happy."

Ron's lips tightened into a straight line. "I don't care where he calls me or what He wants me to do; my life is His from now on."

Danny picked up a pen and worked it mechanically. "You made that decision once before, didn't you, Ron? That time when you had to stay home from high school for a semester and were arrested and taken to Kenora for not having enough guides with that hunting party?"

For an instant the younger boy's face flushed hotly. "I did make that decision once before, Danny," he acknowledged. "But like so many kids, I didn't stay true to it. I got to thinking about all the things I'd like to have, until I began to lose sight of the fact that I had dedicated my life to His service."

They sat up until almost midnight visiting with Harold and Carrie Forester, and for the first night since Roxie's death, Ron was able to sleep quite well. The following morning, about nine, or a little after, Danny and Ron went out to CBI in Mr. Forester's car to pick up Roxie's trunk and suitcase.

Dale Walsh recognized the car and came over to them. "Hi, Ron, I was just going to call you."

Ron questioned him, "Don't you have a class now?"

"That's what I wanted to talk with you about," Dale continued. "We aren't having any classes today. We didn't have any yesterday, either." His eyes lighted. "You'll never believe what's happening here at CBI, Ron. A real revival has broken out! Kids have been getting right with the Lord and with other kids and confessing to their instructors and everyone they have wronged. Dozens have dedicated their lives to Christ, and more are doing it all the time. There were prayer meetings going on until late last night and they started again before dawn this morning. It's the most wonderful thing I've ever seen."

Danny, who was also in the car, stared at the speaker. "What caused it, Dale? Or do you know?"

"The Holy Spirit has used Roxie's death and Ron's confession and testimony at chapel yesterday to touch the hearts of us all. The first response came right after Roxie's death. I think God used that to prepare us for what took place yesterday. Anyway, when Ron told how God had been dealing with him, that seemed to break down the floodgates."

Ron wasn't particularly emotional, but still tears came to his eyes.

"The Lord's been working in other ways, too," Dale continued. "One of the guys went out to help the delivery man unload milk at the kitchen this morning. Before he had a chance to say a word, the man told him that he was tired of living in sin and wanted to be saved. . . . I've never seen anything like it. It's the most wonderful thing I've ever heard of."

Danny and Ron Orlis went up to the storeroom in the girl's dorm and got Roxie's things. Once they had everything, they drove out to the airport in Mr. Forester's car and piled Roxie's luggage into the back of the Cessna 180. They left the car keys with the airport attendant, warmed up the plane, and took off.

The snowstorm that had threatened the day before had given way to a bleak late November sun. It was cold, but there were no clouds in the pale blue sky. When they were three or four minutes out of Fairview, Danny radioed ahead and asked the airport to phone Kay and have her come out to pick them up. At the airport, even before they had landed, Danny spotted their old car.

"Kay's waiting for us, all right," he said. "It looks as though we're not going to have to walk to town."

Ron did not reply.

Tears filled Kay's eyes when she saw Ron Orlis, and she looked away hurriedly to keep him from noticing. She swallowed hard and forced a smile to her lips.

"It's so good to have you with us, Ron. I asked Danny before he left if there was a chance of getting you to come and spend a few days with us. He said he'd try, but he thought you were going back to the Angle to be with Mom and Dad for a time before you go back to your job."

He eyed her squarely. "I'm not going back to my job."

On the way to the house Kay turned to Danny. "Jim will be glad to see you both. He's been wondering if you'd get back in time for Bible club tonight, Danny."

"That's right, I'd almost forgotten that the kids are coming in for club this evening."

Ron's face showed obvious displeasure. "You–you mean you're having company tonight?" Although he tried to mask it, there was a trace of ice in his voice.

Danny and Kay both caught his disapproval. "This isn't a party or anything like that, Ron. It's just that some of the kids from church come in every Thursday night for a little Bible study. It's something like the Bible club we used to have back in Cedarton when we were all going to high school."

Ron nodded, but disapproval still glinted in his eyes.

"Kay and I talked about canceling the meeting tonight, Ron," Danny went on explaining. "If it were a party, neither of us would have considered it. But this is entirely different. This is the Lord's work."

"I know you'll be thrilled by the club, Ron," Kay added. "Jim is the one who got it organized. In spite of the fact that the mission headquarters are located in Fairview, there aren't many Christians in Jim's school. He wanted to do something about it, so he asked us if we'd teach some of the kids from church in a little informal Bible study."

Danny pulled into the driveway and stopped but for the moment did not get out of the car. "There weren't too many kids in Jim's class at Sunday school," he said. "And not all of those who did go were interested in coming over here for Bible club, but there are a few. Just enough to give Jim something to build on. He's been working like everything to get some of the unchurched kids at school to come. Now it seems as though he's just beginning to get some of them interested."

"I'm glad for that," Ron answered. "Believe me,

I am. But couldn't it wait for a couple of weeks? Do we have to have them over tonight?"

"I told Danny that I didn't think I could have company so soon after Roxie's death," Kay told him, "that it didn't seem right to me. But he reminded me that Roxie had dedicated her life to the Lord, and that if she were here, she would be the first to say that we should have the kids come in for Bible study. There may be a chance of reaching one of them for Christ."

The younger Orlis boy did not answer.

Danny touched him on the shoulder. "You see, Ron, regardless of what has happened, we've got to go on living until God calls us home. We've got to go on serving Him."

CHAPTER 2

BASKETBALL HERO HESITATES

Danny and Kay Orlis hadn't expected many kids to come to club that night and neither had Jim Morgan. He had asked a lot of them and quite a number said they would come, but they had promised at other times too. A few minutes before eight the living room was comfortably filled. Kay was hastily putting another cake together when Jim slipped out to the kitchen, eyes alight with excitement.

"Have you looked in there, Kay?" he asked in low tones.

"There are about twice the number of kids I prepared food for, if that's what you mean."

"Boy, I never thought we'd have a crowd like that." He moved closer to her. "Did you know Boyd Patterson's out there."

"Now who is Boyd Patterson?"

"He's the cool kid at school. He's on the basketball team and everything. I don't think he ever goes to church."

"That's wonderful." Kay looked up from the batter she was beating. "Who's that pretty girl who came in about the same time as Boyd did?"

Jim frowned. "Pretty girl? I didn't see any pretty girls out there."

"Oh yes you did. The pretty, dark-haired girl who is sitting on the couch nearest the piano."

"Her." His nose wrinkled. "You ought to know her. She goes to our church all the time. That's Linda Penner."

Linda Penner. Kay turned the name over in her mind. She was Henry Penner's girl. Her mother had died a couple of years or so before.

"I remember her now. She keeps house for her father and her little sister. The poor thing doesn't get out very much."

As soon as Kay finished stirring up the cake and had it in the oven, she went over to where Linda was sitting. "Hello, Linda. I'm so glad you could come tonight."

The girl turned to her. There was a smile on her face but a faint curl to her lips. "I've been hearing about club at school, so I thought I'd come over and–and find out what it's like."

Kay flashed her a quick, friendly smile. "We're so glad you could be with us. I know you'll like it."

"It'll be better than babysitting." Her voice wore an edge. "That's what I have to do most every night, babysit Becky."

The lesson was challenging that night – especially so. Ron didn't come in for the start, but it hadn't been going long when he came in and stood near the doorway, listening. Now and then Danny asked him a question. Ron soon had his Bible open and was participating with the rest, sitting cross-legged on the floor with the kids.

They all listened intently and quite a number hung around for a time after the study was over, visiting and asking questions. Boyd Patterson was among the last to leave. He didn't say much but made no move to go.

"I'm sure glad you could come tonight, Boyd," Danny Orlis said to him. "We sure want you to come back again."

"The meeting was all right, I guess," he admitted with some reluctance. For some reason he seemed to be uncomfortable. A strange light glimmered in his eyes. He swallowed hard and made an attempt or two to speak before the words came out. "Jim was telling me you used to play a lot of football and basketball when you were in high school, Danny."

That wasn't quite what the older Orlis boy expected. It surprised him. "Both Ron and I took part in sports when we were in high school," he replied, "but it seems as though it's been a long time ago."

Ron nodded. "A lot of things have happened since then," he added.

There was a short, uneasy silence. Boyd moistened his lips and cleared his throat, as though there was something special he wanted to ask about, but when he finally did speak, he was still on the subject of sports.

"I play football and basketball," he said, "but I think basketball's my favorite. I'm sure glad we've got started practicing again."

"Going to have a good team this year?" Danny asked.

"I can tell you more about that about the first of March." He went on to ask Danny and Ron about some of the rules they played under when they were in high school and questioned them about fake outs and making jump hook shots.

"Hook shots are my worst weakness," he confessed. "I try and try, but I can't get the hang of them."

"I used to have the same sort of trouble," Ron agreed. "It's easy to understand the fundamentals of a good hook shot. The important thing is to be able to do it – and about the only thing I can tell you is to practice and keep on practicing until you can do it."

"There isn't anything more important in basketball than practice," Danny added. "A person just has to stay at it if he's going to be any good."

Although Boyd continued to ask about basketball, every now and then he stopped, indecision glinting in his eyes. When it was almost eleven, Danny glanced at his watch.

"We've enjoyed having you, Boyd, and we sure want you to feel free to drop back any time you'd like to talk, but don't you think your parents will be worried about you? It'll be almost midnight now before you get home."

Color leaped to the young basketball player's cheeks. His lips parted. "Danny, I–I–" he began, but his voice choked off miserably.

Ron, Danny, and Kay – all three – noticed it.

"Is there something you want to talk with me about?" Danny asked gently.

The flush in Boyd's cheeks deepened to scarlet.

"I–I–I just–" Uncertainly, he got to his feet and started for the door. "Aw, skip it."

Danny followed him. "I don't know whether I can help you or not, Boyd, but if you've got something to talk with me about, I'd sure be happy to try.

The boy's eyes lighted momentarily, then the cloud came back. "It–it wasn't anything." But the question still did not leave his eyes.

"Just give me a ring to be sure I'm home if there ever is any problem you'd like to talk with me about," Danny continued. "You're welcome to come over any time."

It was almost half a minute before Boyd moved.

"I–I've got to be going." With his hand on the doorknob, he looked back. "If I decide I need help on that hook shot, I–I'll probably take you up on that."

Thoughtfully Danny closed the door behind him.

Ron was the first to speak. "That guy's got more of a problem than how to shoot a hook shot," he remarked.

Kay, who had started to gather the trays, looked up. "I think you're right, Ron. That boy troubles me. He acted as though he has something serious on his mind."

"I got the same impression," Danny added. "He acted to me as though he was a guy who's having his troubles but is afraid to say anything about them."

"That's the idea I got," Ron agreed. "If it hadn't looked so obvious, I'd have gotten Kay into the other room. I thought perhaps he didn't want to open up because we were here."

Danny expelled his breath slowly. "That could have made a difference, but I don't know for sure. I gave him every opportunity to tell me that he wanted to see me alone, but he didn't take them."

Danny and Ron both set to work helping Kay clear up the dishes.

"Did Jim ever tell you anything about the boy, Danny?" Ron asked after a time. "Did he ever tell you what he's like?"

His older brother thought for a moment. "I guess he gets along well enough at school, if that's what you mean."

"Do you know whether he has ever had any contact at all with the gospel?" he went on. "Are there any Christians in his family? Does he even go to church?"

Danny shook his head. "I don't know anything about his family, but Jim did say that Boyd has been working at one of the downtown gas stations and garages Saturdays and Sundays, so I know he hasn't been going to Sunday school and church."

Danny took a little notebook from his pocket and made an entry. "I want to be sure to find out just which station he works at and when he works," he muttered, as much to himself as to Ron and Kay. "I think I'll drop in and have a little chat with him the first chance I get."

"I might try to go and see him, too," Ron added, "if I'm here long enough."

"That sounds like an excellent idea, Ron."

There was a short period of silence.

"Danny," Ron finally said, "I'm so glad you had Bible club tonight. I didn't think so at first, but it was the right thing to do."

CHAPTER 3

HOLIDAY SEASON
NOT SO HAPPY

Danny Orlis had to make a trip up to the northern Saskatchewan community of Prairie Lake to overhaul a plane for the mission and asked Ron to go with him.

"I'd like that, Danny," he answered, "but I've been thinking I ought to go back to the Angle to see Mom and Dad. You know, they've been alone ever since Roxie died. I should spend some time with them before I have to go down to Cedarton to start school."

"That's more important than going with me," Danny agreed. 'Why don't I take you by there on my way? It won't be more than half an hour or so of extra flying time and it will give me a chance to see them too."

Mr. and Mrs. Orlis came out on the dock to meet them, as they had done so many times before in years gone by. There were tears in Mrs. Orlis's eyes as she saw Ron, but she wiped them away hurriedly and managed a brave smile. "It's so good to see you boys," she greeted them.

"Yes," Carl Orlis added, "Mom and I were just sitting here wondering when you were going to be coming this way when we saw the plane."

Danny could only stay long enough to have a sandwich and a cup of coffee. In an hour he was back in the air once more. Ron and his parents had been visiting for some time when Mrs. Orlis stopped suddenly.

"You know, Ron, we completely forgot to get your mail for you."

"Mail?" His forehead crinkled. "I wouldn't have any mail up here. No one knew I was coming."

Carl Orlis got to his feet and went into the other room. A moment later he returned with the envelope that was addressed to Ron. "Somebody knew you were here." A wide grin split his face. "And from the looks of that handwriting, it must be a young lady." He handed it to Ron. "Don't tell us you've been holding out on us."

Ron opened it thoughtfully. "This is just from Darlene Snyder," he replied. "She's the girl who used to be Roxie's roommate."

His eyes widened as he read the letter.

"Just listen to this! 'The revival here at school is still going on. Kids are still being convicted of backsliding and are dedicating their lives to Christ's service.

Some have even accepted Christ as their Savior. That sounds unbelievable at a Bible school, but they are kids who were raised in Christian homes and just assumed they were saved because the rest of their families were.'"

"That's wonderful," Carl replied.

Once more Mary Orlis's eyes filled with tears.

"But listen to this. 'Some of us have been thinking about John Porter, the young missionary Roxie was dating. In fact, we talked with Dr. Nielsen about wanting to set up a memorial fund to Roxie and using the money to buy John the plane he needs so much for his work. And, Ron, Dr. Nielsen has okayed it.'"

Numbly Ron stared at his parents, his eyes filling with tears. "Isn't that tremendous?" he asked again.

Mrs. Orlis could contain herself no longer. She cried a little and dabbed at her eyes with the corner of her apron.

"I couldn't understand why God would permit this to happen to Roxie," Ron began after a time, "when she was so concerned about spiritual things and so anxious to serve Him. But now it seems as though God is able to use her death in challenging other Christian young people to holiness and full-time service, far more than he could ever have used her life."

Mrs. Orlis put a work-worn hand on his young arm. "I'm so glad to hear you say that, Ron. You know, the Scriptures tell us, *All things work together for good to them that love God, to them who are the called according to his purpose.* He has called Roxie home, but in doing so He has used her in a very wonderful way."

The corners of the boy's mouth tightened. "I know that's true, Mom."

It was two or three minutes before he could continue. "I saved quite a bit of money when I was working up north. I'm going to put it in the plane fund."

Carl Orlis frowned. "All of it?"

"I'll save enough to live on between now and the time the second semester starts and to pay my tuition for the balance of the year."

"What will you do about your board and room?"

"Work for it, the way most of the other guys do down at school. Don't worry about me, Dad. I can get by. I did before."

Carl Orlis smiled understandingly.

Christmas was approaching and Mary Orlis was busy baking and getting ready for the time when Danny and Kay and Jim would come up. Ron was busy, too. He scooped newly drifted snow out of the path about the place and cut a big pile of wood and piled it neatly just outside the door. Carl Orlis scolded him gently for it.

"You've got enough wood piled up to last us for three years, Ron. You're going to have to put a stop to it or the pile will be bigger than the house."

"When it gets down to about fifty below, you'll be glad you've got it."

Carl Orlis smiled and leaned comfortably back in his chair. "You can say that again. I just don't like to have you work all the time you're here with us."

The light in Ron's eyes died momentarily. "I've got to work, Dad," he said quickly. "It keeps me from thinking." He reached over and stirred the logs in the fireplace until the flames crackled. "If it weren't for the Lord and the strength He gives, I don't know how I could keep going."

Several minutes passed before anyone spoke.

* * *

Danny and Kay and Jim were as busy in Fairview as their parents and Ron were at Angle Inlet. The morning before they were to leave, Danny went into the bedroom where Kay had put out the Christmas packages to pack them. A grin twisted his youthful face.

"You've already got two boxes of stuff packed, Kay," he told her. "If you keep this up, there won't be room in the aircraft for everything."

"There'd better be, or you won't be getting a gift from me. That hasn't been packed yet."

He went over and picked up a package with his parents' names on it. "If these are the Christmas presents," he asked, "what's in that stuff I've already got in the car?"

"I called Dr. Gordon and told him about the Indians on Buckety Island and how badly some of them needed clothing and blankets. He's letting us take them some of the things that have come in to the mission."

Danny put his arm about her shoulder and squeezed her affectionately. "I might have known it was something like that."

He got busy and began to help her. After a minute or two he picked up a package and examined it. "Hey, what's this?" he exclaimed. "How come Ron's getting two packages and I only get one? Is he some special character or something?"

Kay took the package away from him and put it in with the others. "Silly, don't you remember Ron's birthday is next week? I thought we ought to take a gift up to him so we wouldn't have to mail it."

Danny Orlis had made arrangements to rent the mission plane for the trip to Angle Inlet. He had the luggage packed securely aboard, and as soon as Jim Morgan got out of school at noon, they were ready to leave. Jim climbed excitedly into the back of the Cessna 180 and fastened his seat belt.

"I've been watching the clouds out the window all morning. I've been holding my breath for fear it would storm. Wouldn't it have been rough if we'd have had a blizzard today so we couldn't have gone home for Christmas?"

Kay turned to him. "It's going to make a much nicer Christmas for all of us this way."

Momentarily the lights went out of his eyes. "Here I am talking about how terrible it would be if I didn't get to go back to the Angle for just this one Christmas and–and Roxie won't get to go back there again – ever."

His lower lip trembled.

Danny glanced over his shoulder. His face was stern, but his voice was calm and gentle. "I hope you remember not to say things like that to Ron or my parents while we're there. They are going to have to have all the strength God gives them to make this a happy Christmas. We've got to be strong in order to help them to be strong."

"I–I'm sorry, Danny. It popped out before I thought."

They landed at Angle Inlet an hour and a half later. Ron and Jim helped Danny pull the airplane up on bundles of spruce boughs to keep it from freezing down. Before they quit, they tied it securely.

The bitter wind stung Jim Morgan's cheeks to a ruddy hue and played carelessly with the loose snow on the ground. But it was excitement that ignited the dancing fire in Jim's eyes and not the cold. "Have you and Uncle Carl gone out to cut a Christmas tree yet?" he asked.

Ron laughed. "We couldn't trust such an important task to a little kid like you. Finding a good Christmas tree takes an experienced eye. We went out and got it–I went out and got it, personally, a couple of days ago."

Jim sighed. "I figured maybe you already had cut a tree, but I was hoping." He took a deep breath. "Last year Roxie and I–"

Hurt leaped to his eyes, and he choked off suddenly. "I–I'm sorry, Ron. I didn't mean to say that."

Ron Orlis put an arm about the younger boy's small shoulders and gave him a manly squeeze. "That's all right, Jim. I find myself saying things like that all the time." Nevertheless, Ron was very quiet for the next hour or two.

The days at the Angle passed swiftly. Ron and Carl Orlis went over to Buckety Island with Danny and Jim the day before Christmas and distributed the blankets and clothing. When they finished, the chief gave them an opportunity to speak to the people. Afterward two or three came up and asked pointed, searching questions. Ron learned their names and wrote them down.

"I'm going to come back here in a couple of days and talk to them again," he explained.

Carl nodded. "You might have a good chance of reaching some of them with the gospel, Ron. They were showing real interest."

When they got back to the Orlis home, Mary called Danny into the bedroom and closed the door. "Danny, would you mind talking with Ron for your father and me before you leave?"

"Sure I will, Mom. What about?"

"A few days ago, he had a radio message that someone from Iron Mountain, Colorado, wants to reach him by phone, but he won't make the call."

"Why not?"

"He doesn't say, except that he doesn't care to." She breathed deeply. "And this afternoon while you were gone the message came again. It's a lawyer who wants to talk with him, and he says it's very important."

Danny went out and called Ron aside. "Mom tells me that you've had another message about a phone call you're supposed to make."

His younger brother's face grew tense. "I know what it is. It's the lawyer who was handling that trust fund for Roxie and me. I–I just can't talk to him now."

"You'll have to go and see about it."

"But I don't want the money!" His voice was harsh.

"You can do what you please with the money," Danny told him, "but it's your responsibility as a Christian to go make the phone call."

"I suppose you're right."

"If you are determined not to keep the money, there are always Christian groups who find their work seriously handicapped because of a lack of funds. You could make arrangements to give it away or put it in trust and have the interest used for Christian work."

Ron's eyes lighted. "You know, Danny, Roxie would like that, now wouldn't she?"

CHAPTER 4

"I NEVER NOTICED THAT BEFORE!"

Early the following morning Danny Orlis flew his younger brother Ron down to Warroad to take care of some business. As soon as they got back, Danny loaded his wife Kay and Jim Morgan into the plane and headed for Fairview.

Jim sat silently in the rear seat during takeoff. He stared down at the Orlis home for as long as he could see it. "Don't you wish we lived up here still, Danny?" he asked after a moment or two.

"You can say that again."

"There isn't any other place in the whole world that's as nice as the Angle," Jim declared firmly.

"You won't get an argument out of me on that," Danny told him.

"Can't you two find something else to talk about?" Kay asked.

"When I get out of school," Jim said, "I'm going to move into that smallest cabin, on the end down by the creek, and live alone."

Danny laughed. "I used to say the same thing, Jim. And now look at me."

"This has been a wonderful Christmas," Kay changed the subject. "One of the nicest Christmases we've ever had."

It was several minutes before anyone spoke again.

"You know, I've been thinking about Boyd Patterson all day," Danny Orlis said after a time. "Think he'll come to Bible club the next time, Jim?"

"He sure acted like he had a good time. He even talked about it the next day at school."

"I wanted to get over and see him but didn't have a chance before Christmas. You be sure and talk to him about it, will you?"

"I sure will."

"And ask that Penner girl if you happen to see her in the hall, Jim," Kay put in. "I feel so sorry for her."

"I'll ask her," Jim grumbled, "but only so we can get her to Bible club."

"Why else would you ask her?" Danny teased.

"Aw–" His cheeks colored. "You know what I mean."

The next morning Danny accepted delivery of a new courier plane for the mission, and, under the watchful eyes of the company representative, he proceeded to wring it out. As mission pilot it was his responsibility to test it under every conceivable situation to be sure that everything was in perfect working order.

The job still wasn't finished when the night came for Bible club. Danny knocked off work half an hour earlier than usual and got home just as Kay was setting the table for supper.

"Hi, Jim. How's it going? Are we going to have a good crowd for club tonight?"

"I sure hope so."

"Have you been talking it up?"

"A bunch of kids are doing that. Some of 'em really like it."

Danny sat down and crossed his legs. "That makes a guy feel good. What about Boyd? Think he'll be over here tonight?"

"I think so," Jim replied. "I talked with him a couple of times and he said he thought he'd come." He sat down across from Danny. "Boyd said he might be a little late, though. He told me he had to see some guy after basketball practice, and he didn't know how long it would take. But I told him to come anyway – even if he couldn't make it right on the dot at eight o'clock."

"That's the stuff." Danny picked up his Bible and opened it to the portion they would be studying that night. "I sure wish I could get through to that guy."

"What do you mean?" Jim asked. "He likes you. You don't have to get through to him."

"He likes me, all right, but I want to help him and I'm afraid he's not going to let me. At least, he sure shies away. And I'm afraid there's something bothering him."

"Nothing bothers Boyd Patterson." There was a trace of awe in Jim's voice. "And you ought to see him on the basketball floor. Wow, is he slick!"

Although Boyd had told Jim he would probably be a little late in coming to club, he knocked at the door a few minutes before eight o'clock. Danny took his coat and put it in the front bedroom.

"I'm sure glad you could come tonight, Boyd. Jim said he had talked with you and you were afraid you'd be late if you were able to come at all."

Boyd eyed the young missionary pilot uncertainly. "I–I decided I could wait until tomorrow to see the guy I was going to see after practice this evening. It–it wasn't so important, anyway."

Danny showed him into the living room. "It's real good that you got to come. We would have missed you."

They sat down together.

"Ron sure was sorry he had to leave without getting a chance to see you guys play," Danny began. "How's the team coming along, anyway?"

Surprisingly, Boyd frowned and for an instant or two looked away. "All right, I guess. At least we've been lucky enough to win."

Danny exclaimed, "I guess you guys have been winning! I see that you've had five victories in a row to make an undefeated season so far. If you keep playing that kind of ball you ought to be a cinch to go to the state tournament in the Cities, and you might have a chance of going all the way to the championship."

"We've got some good teams to play yet," Boyd said doubtfully. "So far we've just been lucky."

"It doesn't sound like luck to me."

"It's luck, all right," somebody else put in, admiration coloring his voice, "luck by the name of Boyd Patterson."

Danny glanced up at the high school basketballer. Boyd seemed genuinely embarrassed.

"I didn't have much to do with it."

"Not much, you didn't. You're just the high scorer and have been for the last three games."

"The other guys set everything up. I just happened to be the one who got to do the most shooting. It's easy to be a high scorer when everyone else is feeding the ball to you."

"Anyway, Fairview has got a good team," Danny assured him. "I just hope you can keep it going."

"Maybe we will." Uncertainty crept into Boyd's voice. "And maybe we won't. A lot of things can happen between now and tournament time."

There was a knock on the door and Kay went to answer it. Linda Penner came in. She was a slight, pixie-faced individual with black hair and dancing black eyes. Kay ushered her into the bedroom and laid her coat on the bed.

"It's so nice you could come this evening, Linda."

"I stacked the dishes," she explained simply.

They went into the living room and Kay sat down near the door. Linda started to do the same but seeing an empty chair on the other side of Boyd Patterson, she crossed the floor to it.

"Hello, Boyd." There were stars in her eyes and music in her voice.

He looked over at her uncomfortably and grunted. "Hi."

"The way you played last Friday night was–was" she fumbled for words, "was super."

Color came up into his cheeks and he pretended not to hear. Jim Morgan snickered, and Boyd made a face at him.

"I'm so excited about the game tomorrow night that I can hardly wait. How bad are we going to beat them?"

"I'd settle for one point right now," he mumbled. "It's going to be a tough game. We might get skinned."

"Not with *you* playing." She accented the word delicately.

There was no answer.

"Boyd." She smiled at him with her eyes. "I'm going to be there cheering for you."

Kay Orlis broke in quickly, "I wonder if anyone else is coming tonight."

"I don't know." Danny turned to Jim. "How about it? Is there anyone who promised to come and isn't here?"

"Quite a few said they were coming and aren't here yet," Jim answered, "but I told everybody that we would be starting at eight o'clock. I think they'd be here by this time if they were coming."

Danny crossed the room to get his Bible and returned to his chair. "I think we'd just as well get started, then. There's no point in waiting."

When Bible study was over and Kay served snacks, Boyd got his coat quickly and started for the door.

"Do you have to leave so soon, Boyd?" Jim asked him.

He glanced at Linda and then back at Jim. "I sure do," he exclaimed fervently. "I sure do."

The other kids left soon, and Jim turned to Danny and Kay Orlis, disgust clouding his young face. "That Linda!" he exploded. "Who does she think she is, trying to latch onto a guy like Boyd?"

Danny sat down and loosed his shoelaces. "I don't think Boyd minded it. To tell you the truth, I believe he thought she was sort of cute."

"Cute?" Jim's voice raised. "Cute? Danny, are you out of your mind?"

The young missionary stifled a grin.

"I can tell you one thing," Jim went on. "She gets in Boyd Patterson's hair just as much as she gets in mine. He won't have anything to do with her."

"Don't be too sure."

Jim crossed to the kitchen door. "If she keeps on, Danny, she's going to drive him away. That's what she's going to do. She'll drive him away from club."

"Maybe not."

"She would me. If she started after me that way I'd be long gone." Jim grunted. "She's a pain in the neck."

* * *

Two days before the second semester was to begin, Tex Williams flew up to Angle Inlet and Ron rode back to Baudette with him. Ron had planned on taking the bus to Cedarton, but Tex insisted on flying him to school.

"I've got to go to the Cities anyway. You might just as well go along."

It was midafternoon when they touched down at the Cedarton airport. After Ron had phoned for a cab to take him out to school, he stood before the big plate glass window, staring silently out across the bleak, snow-swept airport.

It was nice getting back to Cedarton again. Oh, it would be different with Roxie gone, but deep down in his heart there was real joy and happiness. He was happy to know that he had finally been able to turn his back on the things of this world and give his life completely to God. Happy to know that he was at last in the center of God's will for him.

Ron Orlis was still standing at the window alone, still looking out over the bleak, forbidding, snow-covered fields. He scarcely noticed the car that pulled into the drive and stopped before the small building at the Cedarton airport. He scarcely noticed, that is, until a familiar figure got out.

Dale Walsh! He ran to the door and threw it open. "Dale!"

His tall blond friend came striding over to him and shook hands warmly. "Ron! It's good to see you."

"Darlene and I saw Tex's plane come in and figured you'd be on it."

Ron looked up to see Roxie's former roommate

sitting in the front seat of the old car. She smiled and waved a greeting. He canceled the cab, then he and Dale carried his luggage out to the car.

Darlene Snyder's smile was warm and contagious. "We're sure glad to have you back at CBI, Ron," she told him.

"You aren't half as glad as I am to be back."

The three of them sat in one corner of the dining hall and ate together. Darlene brought Ron up to date on the memorial fund for Roxie. The time passed quickly. It seemed to Ron that Darlene understood about Roxie a little better than anyone else.

They talked about Roxie for a time, about her warm, happy heart, her devotion to the things of the Lord, and the effect of her death on the kids at CBI. It seemed to Ron that they had only been visiting for a few minutes when suddenly it was time for them to go.

On the front steps of the girls' dormitory, Darlene turned and held out her hand. "Thank you for a lovely evening, Ron." Her voice was soft and musical.

He stood motionless until the door closed behind her. Strange, he had never really noticed until that very moment what a lovely girl she was. Thoughtfully he turned and made his way across the campus to the boy's dorm.

CHAPTER 5

"WHAT KIND OF DEDICATION?"

The basketball season at Fairview was well under way. Danny and Kay bought season tickets and became quite regular in attendance except when meetings at church or work at the mission kept them away. Kay liked the game well enough but could not be called a rabid fan.

"If it weren't for Boyd Patterson and the kids in Bible club, Danny," she confessed, "I don't think I would care to go to as many games as we do."

"I like basketball as well as the next one, but I think I'd be at the games even if I didn't care for them at all. Going to high school sports makes such a wonderful contact with the kids."

She pulled up a chair and sat down. "Have you been able to win Boyd's confidence yet? Has he confided anything in you?"

Danny shook his head. "I don't know what the deal is. I stopped by the garage again Saturday morning when they weren't too busy and got to talk with him for a few minutes. But I wasn't able to get anywhere with him." He paused and toyed with a pencil thoughtfully. "He seems to warm up, all right – up to a certain point, but that's as far as he'll go. Then he starts to shy away. There's no chance of getting very friendly with him."

At Bible club that Thursday night Boyd was even more quiet than usual. He came into the house a minute or two before time to start and took a chair near the bedroom door.

Danny Orlis caught his eye. "Hi, Boyd."

The boy's smile was fleeting. "Hi."

"How's the game going to come out tomorrow night? Are we going to win again?"

Boyd hesitated, his lower lip quivering slightly. "We'll have to find out more about that tomorrow night." His tone was a rebuke, but Danny Orlis ignored it.

"I guess you're right at that," he said easily. "From what I hear Bloomingdale has got a hot team this year. Not so strong on defense, but a regular barnburner when it comes to scoring."

Boyd fell silent and stared gloomily at the floor. Others tried to talk with him from time to time, but he said little, answering only direct questions and then as shortly as possible.

Eight o'clock came and they opened the meeting with prayer. They had just finished reading the Bible lesson for the evening when Linda Penner came to the door. Her young face was dark with anger.

Kay led her into the bedroom. "You can put your coat in here if you wish, Linda."

The attractive young girl slipped out of her coat and, standing before the mirror, patted her hair into place. "I'd have been here before," she whined, "but I couldn't get that brat of a sister to help me with the dishes." She paused for a moment. "And Dad told me I had to have them done before I could go anywhere."

Kay looked at her sorrowfully and searched for words.

"Dad about blew a fuse when he came home last Thursday night and found those dirty dishes piled in the sink," she continued.

Kay Orlis paused on her way into the living room. "Danny's waiting for us now, so we don't have time to talk. But why don't you stay a little while after the meeting this evening? I'd like to talk with you."

Linda Penner nodded. She was fighting to keep her lip from trembling. "I've got to do everything around the house," she said, keeping her voice down. "Everything. And if it isn't done the way Mom used to do it, he has a fit."

Kay started for the chair next to Boyd, but Linda got there first. She sat down primly and opened her Bible. Only then did she turn toward the boy sitting next to her.

"Where are we studying this evening, Boyd?"

The line of his mouth narrowed. Without answering, he held his open Bible so that she could see.

"Thank you." Her voice dropped to a murmur and was intended only for him. "It was so late tonight before I got my work finished that I wouldn't even have come if I hadn't known that you would be here."

Boyd's cheeks reddened and he coughed nervously. Linda had intended for her remark to be heard only by Boyd, but Jim Morgan and three or four others close by heard it too. Jim snickered.

Kay Orlis caught Danny's eyes. "It's getting late," she said. "Don't you think we ought to start the lesson?"

The Bible study that evening got off to a shaky start, but after a few minutes settled down until the kids were asking pointed, searching questions. Even Boyd seemed to be clinging to every word and every now and then asked a deep question.

"Is–is that right about God doing what we ask Him to, Danny?" he wanted to know. He tried to sound casual, but there was a tone of urgency in his voice.

Danny Orlis chose his words very carefully. "You can't think of God as being like the genie in Aladdin's lamp who will do anything and everything you think you want," he replied, "but it is true that God promises to answer our prayers. Of course, there are certain conditions that have to be met."

Boyd frowned. "Conditions? What do you mean?"

"The Bible tells us that *the effectual fervent prayer*

of a righteous man avails much. That means we must confess our sin and put our trust in the Lord Jesus Christ for salvation. Then we are righteous through the righteousness of Christ and can claim His promises to answer our prayer."

"You–you mean that you have to be a Christian first?" Disappointment edged his youthful voice.

Danny nodded. "That is exactly right. We have to be the children of God before we can expect Him to hear and answer our prayers." He took a deep breath. "There's something more than that, too. As Christians we've got to be living the way God wants us to. And when we pray, we must pray in accord with His will. Some things we want aren't really good for us, and it may be better if some things we pray for are postponed awhile."

Boyd said no more, but questions were still written across his face.

Kay expected Linda to stay after the others had left so she could talk to her. Linda, however, was the first to get her coat. Kay followed her to the door.

"Do you have to leave so soon?"

Linda's eyes gleamed. "I–I've got to run. I've got to get home before Dad does."

Danny and Kay Orlis sat for a long while in the living room after the Bible club kids had gone home and Jim was in bed.

"You didn't get very far with Boyd Patterson, did you, Danny?" Kay asked.

He untied his shoes and slipped them off. "Not too far. In fact, until the study began and he started asking questions I thought maybe I'd said or done something to offend him, he acted so strangely. But when we got into the study, I could see that he acted that way because he's got something on his mind." Danny leaned back in the chair. "He still acts as though he's got a problem and would like to talk with me about it, but something is stopping him."

"I was very much encouraged tonight during the meeting, though," Kay added. "I thought he was going to show real interest in the things of the Lord. I'll be frank with you, I was disappointed when he didn't go any further with his questioning than he did."

Danny Orlis reached over and picked up his Bible and held it lovingly. "Something's eating at that boy," he continued. "Some real, serious problem, but I don't know what it is."

His young wife came over and sat on the couch beside him. "If only Boyd would talk with us about it, you might be able to help him."

"I even thought of bringing up the subject myself," Danny went on, "but I've been a little afraid to do that. He comes to Bible club now and seems to be interested. As long as he's coming, we have a chance to lead him to Christ. If I make him think I'm prying into his affairs, he might get mad and quit altogether."

* * *

At CBI Ron Orlis found himself in different classes than Darlene Snyder. He was surprised that he noticed it and even more surprised that it mattered to him. But, in spite of that, they seemed to spend a great deal of time together. He began waiting for her in the corridor outside the dining hall so they could eat together and going to the library with her to study two or three evenings a week.

For one thing Ron was comfortable and relaxed around Darlene. He supposed that was one reason he enjoyed her company. She shared the same interests, the same joys, the same disappointments that he did. She was someone to talk to, someone to confide in.

He could mention Roxie and be sure that she would not be embarrassed and uncomfortable or try to change the subject. And when they were together, they often talked about her.

Then there was the memorial fund for the plane. Darlene was one of the originators of the project and was still very active in it. The closer the fund came to reaching the goal, the more work there was to do. Darlene often came to him for advice.

"We almost have money enough to buy the plane, Ron," she told him on one occasion. Her eyes sparkled with excitement as she leaned across the dining table.

Ron smiled boyishly. "That's great."

"We had a meeting of our committee this afternoon. I was appointed chairman in charge of consulting the faculty and arranging for the dedication."

Ron Orlis picked up his fork and toyed with it absent-mindedly. "They couldn't have chosen anyone better qualified for the job than you, Darlene. Why, you've practically promoted this entire project yourself."

She shook her head in protest. "Oh, Ron," she disagreed, "don't ever say that. There are so many others who did much more than I have."

"I know better than that," he answered. "I've been talking with Dale Walsh and some of the other guys. They filled me in on how hard you worked before I got here. And I *know* what you've done this semester."

Darlene flushed delicately. "As a matter of fact," she explained, "it hasn't seemed as though any of us have had to do very much. It seemed as though the Holy Spirit took care of everything for us. As the kids got right with God, the money began to come in and just kept coming."

Ron laid aside his fork with care, and when the words came, they were slow and measured. "That's one of the amazing things about all of this as far as I'm concerned. It still doesn't seem possible that the kids here at school have actually raised enough money to buy a plane for John Porter's mission. It's a real miracle in itself."

Darlene nodded. "That's just the way I feel about it, Ron. There are times when I get excited thinking about what's happening that I have trouble sleeping at night."

They were finishing their dessert before Ron spoke again. "Have you given any thought to the sort of dedication you plan to have?"

"We've done some planning, but we haven't settled on anything definite. That's something I want to talk to you about. Do you have any ideas?"

Ron thought for a moment. "It's hard to come up with anything on the spur of the moment like this, but I got to thinking about something the other night. Have you planned on asking John Porter to come down for the dedication?"

Darlene's eyes lighted. "Do you think he would? We talked about it, but some of the kids thought it was too far for him to come."

"We could find out. If he can possibly leave his work, I know he'd want to come."

There was a short hesitation. "Would you mind asking him about it, Ron? You know him so much better than any of the rest of us do."

"Sure thing. I'll get a note off to him first thing in the morning."

CHAPTER 6

RESOLUTION REAPS RESULTS

As Jim Morgan headed for school the first day after Christmas vacation, Danny Orlis called after the boy. "And remember, Jim, get that information we talked about."

"I'll try."

When Jim got home from school that afternoon, Danny was there making out some reports. As soon as he heard Jim, he came out to the living room.

"Hi, Jim, did you get the information I wanted about Boyd Patterson?" he asked.

Jim took off his coat slowly and hung it in the hall. "I found out some things, all right. The kids out at school all like him and so do most of the teachers."

"I'd have guessed that. He seems like a good boy and has a nice personality. But what's bothering him? That's what I want to know."

The boy went over and sat down. "I don't know

for sure, but I think he's all upset because he might not get to play basketball any more this season."

Danny's frown deepened and it was a moment or so before he spoke again.

"What's the trouble that he might not be able to play? Is it his job? His parents?"

"Oh, it's nothing like that. The talk's going around school that he's having a tough time with his grades and might not be eligible."

"I can't understand that. He gives me the impression of being a good student. And you can sure tell by talking with him that he's smart enough. You must be mistaken, Jim."

"Like I said, that's the talk among the kids at school."

Danny filled his lungs and expelled the air slowly. "He acts to me as though it's something a great deal more serious than that."

Jim's eyes widened. "How could it be any more serious? He's just our best forward and probably one of the best players in the whole conference. How much worse could you want it?"

Danny laughed understandingly. "I just can't see Boyd Patterson with grade trouble, that's all." He got to his feet and went over to the kitchen sink to run a glass of water.

"Some of the kids were saying that the coach and a couple of the teachers and the principal have all been talking to him and they know it must be his grades."

Danny drank the water slowly and set the glass back on the counter. "I think I'll go down to the gas station one of these days and have a talk with Boyd," he said thoughtfully.

"It's going to take more than talk to get Boyd back on the team," Jim retorted. "And if he doesn't get to play, we're sunk."

"I thought he hadn't been kicked off yet."

"He hasn't, but he's going to be. Everybody says so."

Danny said no more to Jim about the young basketball player. However, on Saturday morning when he knew Boyd Patterson was at the garage, he took his car in for maintenance.

"I'd like to have Boyd Patterson do the work," he told the station owner, "if that's all right with you."

"I can put one of the men on it."

"Thanks, but I'd rather have Boyd."

The man shrugged. "Suit yourself. He can go to work on it in a couple of minutes."

When Boyd finished helping another customer, the owner called him to work on Danny's car. While the boy worked, Danny stood around talking to him.

"You've been doing all right on the basketball court, Boyd," he began. "Going to take the conference?"

The boy did not answer.

"What about this outfit you play next Friday night? Are they as good as the news says they are?"

Boyd's eyes darkened and his voice was a snarl. "Don't ask me. Talk to somebody who'll be playing Friday night."

Danny did not show surprise. "Oh, won't you be playing?" he asked. "I thought you really loved basketball."

Boyd put down his tools momentarily and anger fired his eyes. "I do love basketball," he snapped. "It's those crazy teachers who are giving me all the trouble. Just because I'm better at basketball than their little pets, they're picking on me."

Danny stepped backward and leaned against the side of a nearby car. "You sound like someone who's having some grade trouble."

That look came back to Boyd's eyes – an odd look of mingled hurt and indecision, as though he would like to say more, but didn't quite dare. "They'll find out they can't get along without me," he continued defiantly. "If I don't get to play, we'll lose every game."

"I wouldn't get so upset if I were you, Boyd. All you've got to do is get your grades in shape – if that's your trouble."

The thrust was made in the dark, but it struck home. Boyd winced. "I–I can't talk any more, Danny. I've got to get back to work or the boss'll chew me out, but good."

Danny looked at his watch. "You'll be off in a little while. Why don't I stop back and pick you up, Boyd? I'd like to help you if you would only let me."

The boy's lower lip curled. "What makes you think I need help?"

"You've been acting as though you do." Danny had lowered his voice until he was sure no one else could hear him. "You can trust me, Boyd. If you care to share your problems with me, I'll keep your confidence."

Boyd started to speak but checked himself hesitantly. "I–I've got to get to work."

Danny moved to the front of the car with him. "You could come over this evening after work, Boyd. Kay and I would like to be your friends if you'll only let us."

There was a short silence. For an instant or two it looked as though Boyd was weighing the matter, but when he spoke his voice was harsh. "I've already told you. All I've got is grade trouble and those lousy teachers are the only ones who can do anything about it."

Danny's own eyes flashed. "What sort of stuff are you made of anyway, that you'll let a little grade trouble whip you? Anybody who can play basketball the way you do ought to have some backbone."

Defiance blazed in Boyd's eyes, but Danny saw that his lower lip trembled slightly.

"You don't know the half of it," he blurted out.

The young pilot was still not through with him. "I haven't any use for a quitter, Boyd, but if you'd like to have help, Kay and I would be glad to help you get those subjects up where they belong. Kay was on the honor roll most of the time and I managed to get by all right."

There was a short pause.

"Why don't you come over for dinner this evening and we'll go into this grade business. Maybe we can help you so you won't have to quit playing."

Boyd squinted up at him. There was no warmth in his gaze. "Can't make it. I've got to work."

Danny frowned. "That's too bad. How about coming over tomorrow at noon, then? You could go to Sunday school and church with Jim, and we could talk after dinner."

The high school lad hesitated, but there was no mistaking the hurt that flickered in his eyes.

"Sorry, but I can't make it then either," he said. "I've got to work."

"All day?" Danny echoed.

The boy's eyes darkened. "I've got to get in all the time I can. I–I've got a big gas bill I've got to work off."

"Oh," Danny remarked.

"Dad got mad at me, so he won't help pay and I'm stuck." His lips curled, and self-pity twisted his handsome young face. "I suppose he'd be happy if I'd quit school and work all the time," he continued. "That way I wouldn't be costing him anything."

"I don't know your dad," Danny replied evenly, "but I'm sure he would feel terrible if he even heard you say anything like that." He chuckled good-naturedly. "Your dad sounds a lot like mine used to when I was a kid. I bought my own gas and oil, too. Only it wasn't for a car, it was for an outboard motor. I used to call her *Scappoose*."

Boyd's lips relaxed slightly. "I call my old bus *Mary Bell*."

"After a certain friend?" Danny asked pointedly.

The boy laughed aloud. "I guess you could say that. I named it after the meanest, orneriest old cow we ever had when we lived on the farm. She used to kick me half across the barn a couple of times a week."

Danny looked around. "Now you have me interested. Where is this *Mary Bell*? I'd like to take a look at her."

Boyd's eyes narrowed, and for an instant his gaze faltered. "She–she's home."

Danny looked away thoughtfully.

Boyd started to speak but checked himself and swallowed hard. "I've got to get back to work or the boss'll fire me. That'll put me in more trouble than I'm in already."

Danny stayed at the garage until Boyd finished working on the car. He tried several times to get him into conversation, but it was no use. Boyd only grunted or answered with a word. When Danny finally got back to the house Kay was waiting for him, concern dimming the joy that usually glinted in her eyes.

"Well, Danny," she asked, "did you get to talk to Boyd?"

He took off his heavy coat and cap without replying to her question, then crossed the room and sat down wearily.

"I talked with Boyd, all right. He's defiant and close-mouthed, but he's got some problems. You can be sure of that."

Kay went over to the couch and sat beside him. "I've been sure of that. He's acted so strangely the last few times we've seen him—as though he wants to talk to you but doesn't quite dare." She sighed deeply. "I've been praying for him ever since you left." Her eyes searched his. "It didn't go so well, did it?"

He shook his head. "To be frank with you, Kay, it didn't go at all. That boy is as stubborn as a mule. He's in trouble, all right, but he doesn't want to talk about it. He freezes up whenever I try." Danny picked up a pen and held it absent-mindedly as he talked. "Boyd tried his best to make me think that his trouble is in his grades," he continued, "but it's something more than that. Something a lot more." He put down the pen, picked up a magazine as though to read, and laid it down again.

Kay Orlis was the first to speak. "What do you think it is that's bothering him, Danny? Do you think he's in some kind of trouble?"

The youthful pilot looked up. "I don't have the slightest idea. Apparently his dad is punishing him for some reason by not letting him drive his car until he gets his gas bill worked out, but that doesn't sound as though it's a big enough problem to get him all worked up the way he is now."

"Didn't you have a chance to ask him what was wrong?"

"I did." He grinned crookedly. "And I found out that it isn't any of my business. He was friendly enough when we talked about other things, but when I tried to find out what was giving him trouble, he froze up."

Kay reached over and laid her dainty hand on his. "Of course," she said, her voice soft, "the big problem is that Boyd hasn't accepted Christ as his Savior. He could be under conviction."

Danny Orlis nodded solemnly. "He could be, that's true. But I've got a hunch that there's something a little more pressing than that, as far as Boyd is concerned."

That night they spent a long while in prayer for Boyd Patterson.

* * *

At CBI that afternoon Ron Orlis got a large envelope in the mail from Mr. Drake, the lawyer in Iron Mountain, Colorado. He moved to one side and was opening it as Darlene came by.

"My, but that's an important-looking envelope."

His eyes met hers. "It is."

Her cheeks colored delicately. "I–I didn't mean to be prying, Ron. I saw that big envelope and spoke before I thought. I'm sorry."

His smile made her fears vanish. "Forget it. It's just some papers I've got to sign." He looked up at the clock. "Do you have time for a cup of hot chocolate, Darlene? I'd like to talk to you for a couple of minutes."

"I don't have to work this afternoon."

Together they went down to the snack shop in the basement. Ron said little until they had been served.

"These papers have to do with the trust fund our parents had set up for Roxie and me. As soon as I sign these papers and send them back to Mr. Drake, the money will be turned over to me." He spoke without enthusiasm.

Darlene noticed it immediately. "You act as though you aren't very happy about it, Ron."

He picked up the envelope and tapped the table with it, his eyelids narrowing thoughtfully. "Half of this money belongs to Roxie," he told her. "It's not right for me to have it."

Her gaze met his. "Why not?" she asked simply.

He took a deep breath and, laying the envelope aside, nervously ran his fingers through his hair. "Mom and Dad Orlis took us into their home and opened their hearts to us as though we were their very own children," he explained. "Our parents couldn't have loved us any more or treated us any better."

"They're wonderful people."

"You can say that again." He picked up his hot chocolate and sipped it slowly. "They could have gotten money from the trust fund to have paid the cost of raising us and they could have made a little besides, but they didn't do that. They wouldn't take a cent. Now they're older and, Darlene, they don't have any money."

"Perhaps they don't have any money," Darlene smiled, "but they sound very wealthy in other ways."

"They are," Ron acknowledged. "And I think they

are the happiest people I've ever known. But there are so many things they need – things they really ought to have, and probably would have if they hadn't taken the responsibility and expense of raising us." His gaze revealed his concern. "If they could just buy a little house down in Warroad where they could spend the winter months it would be so much easier for them. And they ought to have a car to get around in."

"That would be nice."

"I don't suppose they even have much saved in case one or the other would get sick and have to go to the hospital."

Darlene looked at him curiously. "What are you thinking, Ron?"

He straightened with sudden resolution. "I'm going to do something about that," he declared.

CHAPTER 7

IT TAKES A WOMAN!

Sunday afternoon after dinner Danny and Kay Orlis drove past the gas station where Boyd Patterson was working. Through the window they saw him making change to a customer. Kay suddenly reached over and laid her hand on Danny's arm. "Oh, Danny, let's stop and talk to him a minute."

He glanced down at her, a smile toying with the corners of his mouth. "You never give up, do you?"

She scarcely heard his remark. "That car is leaving now, and he isn't busy. We might be able to talk with him."

Danny drove around the block and pulled into the gas station. "Hi, Boyd," Danny called when they got inside.

Boyd looked up and waved a greeting. "I'll be with you in just a minute."

Slowly he finished what he was doing. At last he gave his attention to Danny. "Need anything?" he asked.

"No, thanks."

Kay leaned toward him. "We just stopped by to see what time you get off work this evening, Boyd."

He eyed her guardedly, and it was a moment or two before he spoke. "I don't know for sure," he hedged. "Sometimes I get off later than I do at other times."

Kay's smile was warm and encouraging. "It won't be too late for you to stop over to our house on the way home and have a dish of ice cream with us, will it?"

He frowned and rubbed his hands together uneasily. "That all depends," he answered warily.

"We don't go to bed very early on Sunday night," she persisted, "and we would like to visit with you. I'm sure you'd have plenty of time to stop at our place for a few minutes after work."

"Well–" He spoke reluctantly. "Well, I suppose I might be able to stop for a few minutes. But I won't be able to stay very long. I–I've got plenty of studying to do."

Kay flashed him a quick, friendly smile. "That's fine, Boyd. We'll be expecting you. Just stop by whenever you can."

When they drove away Danny turned admiringly to his young wife. "Now just how did you accomplish that?" he demanded. "That's what I want to know. I talked with Boyd yesterday until I was afraid he was going to lose his temper and never want to speak to me again. And I still couldn't get anywhere. He turned down my invitations cold." He went around the corner and up the street toward their home. "Just how did you do it?"

The smile left Kay's face. "I didn't do anything but show him that we are interested in him. That's all." She paused. "We've got to make him see that we're his friends and want to help him."

When they got home Jim Morgan was sprawled on the living room floor studying his Sunday school lesson. He looked up when the door opened. "Hi," he said. "Where've you two been?"

"We went for a little ride," Danny told him. "As a matter of fact, we went over to see Boyd Patterson."

Jim scowled. "That guy!"

Kay Orlis frowned her disapproval. "I thought Boyd was a friend of yours," she replied.

Jim closed his Sunday school lesson and sat up. "He is a friend of mine, but I get so disgusted with him sometimes that I don't know what to do." He looked from Danny to Kay and back again. "Know what happened? His grades were going along great until just before Christmas. Just when we started playing basketball and needed him, he started goofing around or something. Anyway his grades really took a nosedive." Jim made a helpless little gesture.

"How come?" Danny wanted to know.

"Search me. We all wanted to try to help him get his subjects in shape – the coach, the principal, the teachers, and everybody. But it hasn't done a bit of good. They keep getting worse and worse all the time. Now, he's going to be kicked off the team, and it's all his own fault."

Danny reached over and straightened a magazine on the table. "He was telling me about it yesterday."

Jim's eyes brightened at the information. "Do you think you can help him so he can play again, Danny?" he asked. "Do you?"

The youthful pilot tugged at the lobe of his ear. "I guess maybe he does have some grade problems, Jim, but I think they're minor as far as Boyd is concerned."

"What do you mean by that?"

"I don't know just what I mean," Danny admitted. "But I do know that Boyd's got some real problems he doesn't want to tell anyone about." He breathed deeply. "So, I'm afraid there's nothing much that anybody can do to help him right now, except to pray."

For a long while Jim was silent. "Know what's the matter with that guy?" His eyes lighted suddenly. "He doesn't have the Lord Jesus to help him."

Danny nodded. "You know, I think you're right."

"I know I'm right. I remember how I used to be before I confessed my sin and accepted Christ as my Savior. I was the same way. I didn't want to trust anybody."

Danny's eyes met Jim's. "Have you ever talked with him about the claims that Christ has on his life, Jim?" he asked suddenly.

The Morgan boy flushed. "I–I've talked with him about coming to Bible club," he replied, "and I've asked him to go to church and Sunday school with me."

Danny's gaze held his. "That's not the same."

"I–I guess I really haven't talked with him about

the Lord Jesus, Danny," he confessed. "I–I guess I've been afraid that he would think I was old-fashioned or something."

Danny Orlis took a deep breath. "There are worse things than being known as old-fashioned, Jim," he remarked simply. Crossing his legs, he leaned back in the chair. "If we had witnessed to Boyd as we should, there's a chance that he would be a Christian now and have these problems of his – whatever they are – solved. Then he'd have his grades up and be playing basketball."

Jim Morgan was a long while in speaking. "You know, I'd never thought of that."

That evening Danny, Kay, and Jim went to church as they always did on Sunday night. However, they were a little slower than usual in getting away that evening, and when they got home Boyd Patterson was just coming down the walk.

"Look," Jim exclaimed. "There's Boyd!" He got out of the car and ran up to his friend. "Hi, Boyd. We've been looking for you."

"I was beginning to think there wasn't anyone at home," he declared. "I was just about ready to leave."

Danny Orlis laughed good-naturedly. "We were afraid you might get over here and be gone before we got home ourselves."

They went into the house and Kay Orlis made her way directly to the kitchen to fix snacks, taking Jim Morgan with her. Danny Orlis and Boyd Patterson were left alone together.

"I'm real glad you came over, Boyd," Danny told him.

The boy said nothing.

"I don't want to pry," Danny continued bluntly, "but I've been watching you, Boyd. There is something troubling you. Something quite serious. I'm going to tell you once more that if there's anything we can do to help, we'll be happy to."

Boyd took his jackknife from his pocket and began to fumble nervously with the blades. "It's too late for you to help me now," he mumbled. "There's nothing anybody can do."

Understanding showed in Danny's eyes. "Now, Boyd, don't be too sure of that. It would have to be quite a problem if it was something that nobody could help you with."

Boyd's eyes flashed hotly. "It is!"

He took a deep breath, opened his mouth, and the words tumbled out with a rush. "The cops in this town have got it in for me. All they do is follow me around trying to get something on me."

Jim came into the room just then and Boyd colored deeply, and his words choked off in mid-sentence.

Danny looked up. "I think you had better turn in, Jim."

The Morgan boy stiffened. "But, Danny," he protested, "we're just going to have some food."

Danny said no more, but his eyes met Jim's the way his own dad used to look at him when he protested a decision. Kay put her arm about the boy's shoulders, but she spoke to Danny.

"Will it be all right if Jim eats with me in the kitchen?" He nodded.

When Kay and Jim were gone and the door was closed behind them, Danny turned to his troubled guest once more. His voice was quiet, but insistent.

"What makes you think that the authorities have it in for you, Boyd?" he asked.

The boy's temper flared. "I don't think they have it in for me," he exploded. "I know it! You just watch them sometime if I'm around." He took a deep breath and pushed it forcibly from his lungs. "If I drive past a cop on the street, he'll turn around and tag me, just trying to catch me at something."

Danny meditated. "I see," he finally replied. "You've been having car trouble." He spoke quietly and without condemnation. "I understand a lot of guys your age have the same problems."

"Not as bad as I have. I've got 'em all! A whole mountain of them!"

"Would you like to tell me about it?"

"I don't know why," Boyd answered. "I don't even know why I've told you as much as I have. There's nothing you can do."

"Sometimes it helps just to talk."

"Anyway," Boyd continued, anguish welling in his voice, "anyway, I had a little accident and that got the cops on me."

"Now wait a minute," Danny broke in. "There had to be something more than just an accident. A lot of people have accidents, and the authorities never bother them."

"Well–" The boy's cheeks reddened. "They had picked me up for speeding a time or two, then they claimed I ran a red light when I had the accident and–and the roof fell in." It was a moment or two before he could continue. "The insurance company canceled my insurance, and Dad wouldn't pay my gas bill at the station, and he–he won't even let me drive my car." His voice choked.

"I can understand that," Danny remarked.

"Now they're going to try me for running that red light and hitting that other car and–and I'll lose my driver's license and it'll be in the paper and everything. Everyone at school will know about it."

Danny's eyes met his. "You apparently haven't been driving your car for some time. Haven't the kids at school known that?"

Color faded from Boyd's cheeks. "I–I told them that I'd blew a head gasket and–and didn't have the money to get it fixed," he confessed hesitantly.

Danny Orlis uncrossed his legs and leaned forward slightly. "You know that the authorities have their job to do, Boyd," he reminded him. "If you hadn't broken the law, you wouldn't be in the trouble you're in now."

"A lot of guys drive faster than I do."

"That's no excuse."

"But I'm the one who got caught," he moaned. "And now all the kids at school will find out about it. I'll never be able to face them again."

Danny nodded his understanding. "That's the way it is with sin," he explained. "A guy starts out doing something he shouldn't be doing in secret. He figures that no one will ever find out about it. But he's wrong. Sin has a way of coming out and sooner or later everyone knows."

Boyd leaned forward, intently. "I don't know what's the matter with them. I've been down and talked and talked to them about giving me another chance. I've promised that I won't do it again, but it hasn't done a bit of good." His eyes flashed at the thought. "The only way I can figure is that they all have it in for me. They finally caught me and they're going to give me as rough a time as they can."

"You're wrong about that," Danny countered. "The authorities don't have it in for you. Nothing would please them more than to have you start driving in such a way that they would never have to stop you."

"Then why don't they try me just this once? Why don't they give me a chance to show them what I'll do?"

"They've been given the responsibility of enforcing the law, Boyd. You've broken the law. They can't close their eyes to that."

The Patterson lad straightened up. "You're just as bad as the rest of them!" His voice raised. "You've got it in for me, too!" He got to his feet and started for the door. "And you have been trying to kid me into thinking that you want to be a friend of mine – that you want to help me! That's a bunch of baloney!"

CHAPTER 8

"I'LL FACE THE MUSIC!"

Danny Orlis followed Boyd Patterson to the door. "Just a minute, Boyd," he spoke firmly. "I'd like to talk to you."

"I don't want to talk to you."

"You're going to talk to me anyway. Do you know the big thing that's bothering you right now?" he demanded.

"Sure." The boy turned to face him. "I'm going to lose my driver's license."

"You think that's the reason," Danny told him quietly, "but it's not. Not really. The thing that really bothers you is pride. You're concerned about what the kids at school will say. You don't want them to know that you got caught speeding."

Boyd bristled. "I thought you wanted to help me, but like I said, I see that you don't. You're just like all the rest of them. You want to pick on me, too."

"I do want to help you," Danny disagreed, "but it's not easy for you to accept help. You're sort of like a guy with a broken leg. You wouldn't say the doctor didn't want to help you just because setting the leg happened to hurt a little, would you?"

The boy fell silent.

"Pride and disobeying the law and all these things are really symptoms of something else, Boyd," Danny continued. "They are symptoms of a life that is being lived without God – a life that is given over to sin." He leaned forward slightly. "Tell me, have you ever considered your personal relationship with the Lord Jesus Christ?"

Hurt flashed in the high schooler's eyes, and he could not look directly at Danny.

The youthful pilot opened his Bible to chapter 53 of the book of Isaiah and slowly began to read the verse he knew so well.

"*All we like sheep have gone astray; we have turned every one to his own way; and the Lord hath laid on him the iniquity of us all.* Boyd, that applied to me and to Kay as well as it does to you. Each person who has ever lived, or ever will live, comes under that verse. None of us are righteous. No, not one."

The boy clenched his fists until his knuckles whitened. "I didn't know you were going to preach to me," he muttered, "or I wouldn't have come over here tonight at all."

Danny ignored his remark. "The book of Romans tells us *the wages of sin is death; but the gift of God is eternal life through Jesus Christ our Lord. . . .* So, although we have each sinned and sin is worthy of death, God has provided a way for us to escape. He sent His only Son to live a perfect life before us and to die on the cross and be raised again so that we can be saved."

Boyd's thin lips tightened. "Just what has that to do with me losing my driver's license?" he demanded. "That's what I'd like to know."

"Everything," Danny replied evenly. "You are losing your license because of the sin in your life. And sin is the one thing that is causing you to keep it from the kids at school. There's just one thing wrong with you, Boyd. You're just like Nicodemus. You need to be born again."

He continued to present the plan of salvation to the young guest, outlining it step by step.

At last Boyd Patterson raised his gaze to meet Danny's. Emotion tightened the muscles in his face, and his eyes were luminous with tears. "I know that what you've said is true, Danny. I–I want to be saved."

"That's fine," Danny Orlis told him. "How badly do you want it?"

Boyd frowned. "What do you mean?"

"Just this. You might listen to me and get to thinking that it would be nice to be a Christian. You might think that you probably wouldn't have any more problems, or that somehow God would miraculously work out everything in your life that is bothering you. There's only one reason you can accept Christ as your Savior. That is because you know that you are a sinner and trust Christ to save you. It's really a simple thing, but you've got to mean business with God."

He paused momentarily. "That's the only basis on which God is going to work. He isn't going to miraculously cause the driving charges against you to be dropped. He isn't going to make the insurance company reinstate your policy or convince your dad that he ought to pay your gas bill. He probably won't even keep some of the kids from looking down on you when they find out what's happened. Those things have come about as the result of sin and the chances are you are going to have to pay the full price for them."

Boyd Patterson nodded his complete agreement. "I know all that, Danny. But it doesn't make any difference."

"That's fine. One thing God is insistent on is the right motive. You've got to be serious in wanting to become a Christian to be rid of the consequences of sin. If you mean business with God and want to be saved and to live for Him, then He will save you and will give you the strength to take the loss of your driver's license and all that goes with it."

There was a long silence. When Boyd Patterson finally spoke again, his voice was taut and hushed. "I am serious, Danny, as serious as I've ever been about anything in my life. I want what you and Kay and Jim have."

Together they knelt on the living room floor and Boyd Patterson gave his heart to Christ.

When they finished praying Kay Orlis came in.

"Kay," Danny said, "I think that Boyd has something he wants to tell you."

The boy's face was flushed, and his eyes sparkled brightly. Still the words did not come as readily as they usually did. "I–I just became a Christian, Mrs. Orlis. I–I accepted Christ as my Savior."

Suddenly Kay's eyes filled with tears. "Why Boyd, that's wonderful." She sat down opposite him.

"I think it is, too."

"Tell me," she continued after a moment or two, "do you have a Bible?"

"I've got one around somewhere, I guess. My grandmother gave it to me for Christmas a couple of years ago."

Kay got to her feet and started toward their bedroom. "I'm going to give you a Bible so you'll have something to use until you find yours," she told him.

"That's a good idea," Danny broke in. "Reading the Bible regularly is an absolute must if you're going to live a Christian life."

For an hour or more the young married couple sat on the couch with Boyd, one on either side of him, marking verses in the Bible and explaining about the Christian life. It was after eleven o'clock when he finally rose to leave.

Danny Orlis followed him to the door. "We'll be praying for you," he promised quietly.

"Thanks. Thanks a lot." Boyd beamed. "This has been the most wonderful day in my whole life."

* * *

At CBI Darlene Snyder and her committee had set the date for the dedication of the mission plane and mailed out invitations. As she and Ron Orlis sat together in the lounge, she brought him up to date on what was happening.

"It's going to be one of the biggest events that's ever been held here at CBI, Ron," she cried excitedly. "You ought to see the response we're getting to our invitations and they haven't been out a week yet. Everyone who can possibly come is going to be here."

"I know. Kay said that Marilyn and Chuck Martin are going to be coming. And of course John Porter will be here, and Danny and Kay and our parents. It's going to be a wonderful time."

"I've been so glad that John decided he could come. It wouldn't seem right to have it without him."

"I knew he'd come if he could," Ron answered.

He picked up the folder describing the plane they were buying and began to read it thoughtfully. "The plane is the thing that interests me, Darlene. When can we get delivery? And do you know for sure that it will be here in time for the dedication?"

Darlene nodded. "Dale talked with the salesman this morning. He said they have to finish overhauling the engine, but that it should be ready to fly by the end of the week."

"Did I tell you that Danny will go down to

Minneapolis and get it for us? He said he thought he could land in that field behind the administration building if they'll put the plane on skis."

Another couple came in from outside and, sitting on a couch nearby, spoke to them. For a few minutes Ron and Darlene talked with them about the weather and the tests they were having in Christian Living the next day.

After a time, Ron turned to Darlene. His lips parted as though to speak. Then he glanced up at the kids nearby and glanced at his watch. "There's still an hour or so before you have to be in your room, Darlene. How about going for a walk with me?"

She would have protested, but something about the look in his eyes stopped her. "I'll get my coat."

In a moment or two they were ready and went out into the frigid night air. Darlene waited for Ron to speak. They crossed the campus to the library, turned, and made their way toward the chapel.

"I was going to tell you this inside a few minutes ago, Darlene," he began once they were alone together. "But then I got to thinking that Pete and Sue would hear me and maybe would get the wrong idea about what I was saying."

She eyed him curiously. "I thought you must have something you wanted to tell me."

Ron stopped and turned to face her. "I probably shouldn't even be telling you this, either," he admitted, "but somehow, I'm sure that you'll understand."

Her gaze met his. "I'll try."

Ron grinned self-consciously. "You know, Darlene," he blurted, "I feel more comfortable and at ease around you than I have with any girl I've ever dated." He paused momentarily. "And, to tell you the truth, I feel a lot closer to you in so many, many ways."

She colored delicately. "Thank you, Ron." Then she laughed. "Is that what you asked me to come out here to tell me?"

"Not exactly. I was just going to tell you that Danny and I have been doing quite a bit of corresponding about the plane you are getting for John Porter. It's a fine airplane. A Cessna 180. It's the real workhorse of the far north."

"We checked with the mission before we bought the plane to be sure it would be the best suited for the purpose. The plane's used, but it has a new aircraft guarantee." She shrugged her shoulders. "I don't really know anything about it, but that's what Dale and the other guys on the committee have been telling me."

"It doesn't make any difference whether a plane has been used or not if it hasn't been badly wrecked. That isn't what I'm getting at. Danny said it would be nice if they could have better radio equipment, new floats, and a number of other items that would make for safer, more trouble-free flying. I don't intend to say anything about this to anyone except you, but when I get that money from the trust fund I'm going to have Danny buy the accessories they ought to have."

Darlene Snyder's eyes grew misty. "Oh, Ron!" she exclaimed. "That's wonderful!"

CHAPTER 9

"NOW I'VE HEARD EVERYTHING!"

The following day after Boyd Patterson accepted the Lord Jesus Christ as his Savior, Jim Morgan stopped by the Patterson home on the way to school. His friend was just about ready to leave.

"I was going to stop at your place this morning, Jim," Boyd said, getting into his coat. "I wanted to talk to Danny about something."

"It wouldn't have done you any good. He's already gone. Had to fly someone up to Canada and won't be back for a couple of days."

Boyd's frown deepened. "You mean he won't be back?"

"Oh, he'll be back, all right – he's nearly always back before Sunday. Why?"

"Oh, nothing. I just wondered if he'd go some-where with me, but he can't make it now."

Jim walked in silence beside his friend for half a block or more.

"Did Danny tell you that I accepted Christ as my Savior last night?" Boyd asked after a time.

"That's why I came by to see you this morning. That's great. You'll never be sorry you did."

"I know that already." There was a brief silence. "If I'd known how wonderful it is to be a Christian, I'd have done it a long time ago."

They crossed the street.

"Danny told me that I ought to tell my parents about it," Boyd continued. "I tried to talk with them this morning, but it didn't do any good. They didn't have any idea what I was talking about." Boyd stopped on the walk.

"Don't feel so bad about that," Jim encouraged him. "It was a long time after I became a Christian before my dad was saved." Sorrow dulled his eyes. "Mom doesn't know Christ as her Savior yet."

But his companion had something else on his mind. A moment or two later he continued. "Did–did Danny tell you about the trouble I'm in?" he asked.

Jim shook his head. "Danny would never tell anybody anything that's a secret. If you told him something, you can know it's not going to be spread all over town."

Briefly Boyd told Jim about being arrested for speeding and reckless driving and that he was about to lose his license. "And I thought maybe Danny would go up to the judge's office with me tonight after school. They're going to have the trial today."

Jim thought a moment. "That is too bad. Danny would be glad to go with you." The look on his face changed. "But it wouldn't do any good for him to be there, I can tell you that much. He wouldn't try to get you out of it."

"I don't want to get out of it," Boyd responded quickly. "I broke the law and I–I know I've got to pay the penalty, even if it means that I've got to lose my license for a while. But I–I thought maybe he would go up there with me – just so I wouldn't have to–to be alone."

"Oh, he'd do that, all right, and be glad to."

When they got to school one of the guys on the basketball team, Scott Decker, came up to him. "Say, Boyd," he cried excitedly, "what's this we've been hearing about you?"

The Patterson boy colored.

"Are you really losing your driver's license?"

"Where did you hear that?" he asked.

"My dad heard it Saturday uptown. What I want to know is, is it true? Are they really going to ground you?"

He squared his shoulders and looked his questioner squarely in the eye. "It's true, all right."

Scott eyed Boyd strangely, as though he hadn't expected him to confess so readily. "That's tough. Those lousy cops around this town! When they get it in for a guy they never do ease off."

Boyd swallowed hard. "I don't know that I can blame the cops," he answered. "If I hadn't broken the law, they wouldn't have arrested me."

Scott stared at him. "What's the matter with you, Boyd? Are you crazy or something?"

"It's the truth. The way I was driving I was just asking for trouble."

"I never thought I'd hear you say that."

"I didn't think I'd ever say anything like that," Boyd admitted, "but my life is changed. I'm different than I have been."

By this time half a dozen guys had joined the little circle.

"What do you mean by that?" Scott asked.

"I'm different," Boyd repeated. "I've confessed my sins and have given my heart to Christ. I'm a Christian now."

Scott Decker's eyes widened. "You're kiddin'!"

"I'm telling you the truth."

"Now I've heard everything!"

One by one the guys drifted on up the corridor. When Jim and Boyd were finally alone, Jim turned to him.

"Hey, that was great! It takes a lot of nerve to tell your story that way."

The other lad smiled his relief momentarily. "Know something, Jim, I've actually been dreading coming to school this morning. I'd have given anything if I could've skipped it."

"Because of the trial tonight?"

"I guess that did bother me a little, but there was something else that hit me harder than that. I knew some of the guys would come up and start talking to me this morning. The story of my being arrested has really spread all over town. I knew they'd ask me about it, and I'd have to give them my testimony."

"You sure didn't act as though it bothered you," Jim told him.

"It wasn't nearly as bad as I thought it was going to be–especially after I got started."

They reached the stairs Boyd had to go up to get to his homeroom.

"I–I'll be praying for you tonight," Jim told him.

"Thanks." Boyd started to leave but turned back. "Jim, I–I hate to ask you this, but would you–would you go up to the courthouse with me?"

The younger boy stared at him in amazement. "Do–do you really want me to?"

"I sure do." Hurt leaped to his eyes. "Oh, skip it. Just because I have a problem is no sign you've got to take your time. I'll be seein' you."

Jim ran and caught him. "Listen, if you'd like to have me go along, I–I'd be real proud to do it. Honest, I would."

Their eyes met.

"You are a friend."

It seemed to Boyd and Jim that school would never end that afternoon, but finally the bell sounded, and the kids jumped to their feet and began to funnel out to their lockers. Jim waited for Boyd on the lower landing. Their eyes met, but neither spoke until they were outside.

"You–you don't have to go with me if you don't want to," Boyd's voice trembled.

"But I want to," Jim protested.

A full minute passed.

"I asked my dad about going with me, but he said that I got into this mess and – that I've got to get out of it myself."

They crossed the street and cut through an alley.

"What do you think they'll do to you?" Jim asked.

Boyd shook his head. "I don't know. They could get awful rough if–if they want to."

"They won't put you in jail or anything like that, will they?"

Boyd stopped short as though he had never thought of that. "Now that's a happy thought."

They went into the courthouse and up to the judge's chambers. The arresting officers were already there.

Boyd wiped his forehead with a trembling hand. "You'll be praying for me, won't you, Jim?" he whispered.

His companion nodded.

As soon as Judge Marshall saw that everyone was present, he asked the county attorney to read the complaint.

"Well, Boyd," he said, leaning forward and tapping the bench with his glasses, "you've heard the complaint against you. How do you plead?"

It was a moment or two before Boyd could bring himself to speak, but when he did his voice was firm and clear. "Guilty, Your Honor."

The trial didn't last long. Judge Marshall asked the officers to tell what happened and Boyd agreed with their story.

"I have no alternative, Boyd," the judge declared, "except to suspend your driver's license for a period of six months."

In a few minutes the trial was over, and they were outside once more.

"I'm sure glad I don't have to go through that again!" Boyd Patterson exclaimed.

"It's going to be tough losing your driver's license for six whole months."

"It sure is," he answered, "but it's like the judge said, I did deserve it. I knew better than to drive the way I was doing. They'd warned me plenty, but I wouldn't listen." There was a short silence. "I sure am anxious to talk to Danny about something. When did you say he'd be back?"

"He ought to be home tomorrow night," Jim replied, "Why?"

Boyd kicked a piece of ice with the toe of his boot. "I've got something I must ask his advice about. I didn't even think of it until this afternoon."

Jim eyed him curiously but asked no questions.

"You know when–when this thing first started to pop, I told you that I was having grade trouble."

Jim nodded. "It seemed funny to me," he admitted. "I'd always heard you were a good student."

"It wasn't true," Boyd went on, "but I figured I

was going to have all the kids in school thinking it was. I–I thought that would be better than having them know the truth."

"What do you mean by that?"

"I found out tonight that it wasn't true, but I'd heard that if the judge suspended my driver's license the school wouldn't let me play basketball until the suspension was over. The guy who told me said it was just like being on parole." He swallowed hard. "I–I was so proud I didn't want anybody to know about losing my license. I–I thought it was better if they thought I couldn't play because my grades were low. So that's why I started the story."

They walked on for half a block or so. "What did you figure Danny could do about that?" Jim Morgan asked at last.

Boyd shrugged his shoulders. "I really didn't think he could do anything about it. I–I just wanted a little advice. I want to find out what he would do if he were in my place." His mouth firmed. "Now that I'm a Christian I want to get everything in order. If Danny thinks I ought to go to anyone and apologize and tell them I'm sorry for having lied to them, I'll do it."

Jim thought for a minute. "That's a tough one. I don't know what Danny would say. But I can tell you this much, Boyd. You're sure on the right track. Danny says God can really work in a life that's completely dedicated to Him."

"I found out what it's like to live for myself," the

new Christian went on. "If I'd accepted Christ as my Savior before, I'd be driving my car now and wouldn't be in this mess."

They were almost at his house when Jim spoke again. "There's something else I've wondered if you ever thought about, Boyd. What about that Sunday job of yours?"

Boyd stopped and turned to face his companion. "Why?"

"It keeps you from attending church and Sunday school for one thing," Jim explained. "That's going to make a big difference in whether you grow spiritually or not."

"But I've got to have a job."

Jim Morgan said no more to him, but when they reached the place where they parted, Boyd mentioned it himself.

"I'm going to pray about it," he declared, "and ask God to show me whether I ought to work Sundays or not."

CHAPTER 10

"WHO WILL GO FOR US?"

The following night Danny Orlis came in from Canada, so Kay Orlis and Jim Morgan went out to the airport to get him. On the way home he asked about Boyd Patterson and what had happened Monday.

"You should've heard him, Danny," Jim cried. "He hadn't been in the school ten minutes before he had told some of the kids that he was now a Christian."

"That sounds good. Whenever a new convert starts to tell his salvation story you can be pretty sure that he means business," Danny said. "And I don't know of anything that will strengthen him more than talking about his faith."

"He means business, Danny, and he'll tell anyone. I've never seen anyone like him. When he was in court yesterday afternoon, he gave his testimony to the judge and apologized to the arresting officers for giving them such a bad time when they picked him up."

Danny turned the corner and slowed to a stop in front of their home. "That is good news." He reached down and switched off the engine. "But what did happen in court? As far as the trial went, I mean? Did they fine him?"

"The judge suspended the fine but took his driver's license from him for six months."

"That sounds very fair." They got out of the car and started for the house. "He broke the law. He should have been punished for it. The way he likes to drive there isn't anything they could do to him that would hurt him worse."

Jim thought for a moment. "You know, Danny, Boyd acted as though he was glad they had taken his license from him."

"Now wait a minute, Jim," Danny cautioned, "that's going a little far. Boyd likes that old car of his just as much as he likes his right arm. He wouldn't be happy that they made him stop driving."

"Oh, he's going to miss getting to drive, all right. What he meant was that getting into this mess over driving and knowing he was going to lose his license for a while was the thing that made him stop and think about himself and where he was headed. He said he didn't think he would have accepted Christ as his Savior if that hadn't happened."

Danny Orlis nodded. "He may have something at that."

Bible club that week was the best they had ever

had. Boyd Patterson gave his testimony to the kids, and they all listened intently.

"I've got to ask you kids to forgive me for lying to you," he began. "I lied about having grade trouble because I thought I'd keep you from finding out what really was going to happen to me. It was pride that made me lie to you. Just as it was pride that made me want to run my own life. But that's all over now. I've confessed my sin and have put my trust in the Lord Jesus Christ for salvation. With His help I'm going to live for Him." Boyd took a deep breath. "If any of you guys want to buy gas from me, you're going to have to come to the station on Saturday. I'm not going to be working on Sunday any more. I'm going to be in Sunday school and church where a Christian belongs. . . ."

When Boyd finished his testimony, a hush settled over the kids and they didn't stick around long after the meeting was over. When they were all gone home Danny Orlis turned to Kay.

"Did you see the way those kids were listening?" he asked. "If we can get them like that next week, we ought to have a good chance of leading some of those kids to Christ."

"Danny, I don't know if I've ever been as delighted as I am right now," Kay bubbled. "Wasn't that testimony of Boyd's marvelous?"

"It really was. That boy's going to grow."

"He's already farther along than some of the kids who have been Christians for several years."

"You can say that again." Then Danny's face grew even more serious. "But that doesn't mean that Boyd's got it made – that we can expect him to walk as a mature Christian. We're going to have to keep working with him and praying for him."

* * *

Two days before the plane was to be dedicated at Cedarton Bible Institute, Danny Orlis went down to Minneapolis and flew the newly acquired Cessna 180 up to Cedarton where he landed on the snow-covered field near the administration building. Students saw him come in and, recognizing the plane, flocked out to meet him. Ron Orlis and Darlene Snyder were among the first.

"Hi, Danny," Ron sang out, hurrying forward with his hand outstretched. "I see you made it."

Danny got out of the plane and came to meet them. "It sure is good to see both of you."

Danny then turned and stepped back to survey the plane critically. "You people made a good buy, Ron. It's one sweet little airplane."

"That's what the salesman told us. He said it was a plane he could recommend all the way. He said that it's as clean as any used plane he sold in the past five years."

"It's a good, serviceable plane," Danny repeated. "It ought to be a big help to John Porter and the mission."

By this time fifty or so students were swarming about the sturdy little craft, examining it with pride and admiration.

Danny glanced about. "Tell me something, Ron," he asked, "what are we going to do to keep everyone from seeing it before the dedication ceremony tomorrow?"

His younger brother glanced Darlene's way, a smile crinkling his face. "That's out of my department," he answered. "It is Darlene's baby." His voice raised triumphantly. "I'll bet that's something you didn't think of, Darlene."

She made a face at him and pointed in the direction of one of the buildings. Several guys were coming out of it carrying a heavy tarp out to a pickup.

"Somebody thought of it," she countered. "Those guys ought to be over here in about two minutes. They're going to help stake out the plane and cover it with the tarp so no one else will get a good, close look at it until the dedication."

Ron shook his head. "I tell you, Danny," he admired, "I've never seen anyone like Darlene. She must be able to see into the future because she thinks of everything."

"I just happened to have a good committee," she answered modestly.

"You know better than that. Half the ideas originated with you."

"Is there any more we can do out here?" she asked. "I'm freezing."

Danny spoke up quickly. "Why don't you take Darlene back to the dorm, Ron? There's no need for both of you to stay out here while the plane's being staked down."

"I'm really not in that big a hurry to get back," Darlene explained.

"Why don't you go on back, Darlene?" Ron suggested. "I'll stay and help Danny."

But his older brother wouldn't hear of it. "There's no need for you to stay out here and freeze. Go on in where it's warm. That's what I'm going to do just as soon as I get this job finished." He took hold of Ron's arm and gave him a little push in the direction of the buildings. "Now get along. I can stake down a plane without help from the likes of you."

* * *

Boyd Patterson went over to Danny's house the evening the young pilot was in Cedarton delivering the plane.

"Danny isn't here, Boyd," Kay called out, smiling warmly, "but Jim is. Come in."

He stomped the snow off his heavy boots and unzipped them. "I can't stay more than a few minutes. I just came by to talk to Danny. I–I wondered if he would help me with something."

She ushered him into the living room. "I'm sure he would if he were here, Boyd. Is there something I can do for you?"

"I–I don't know for sure." He shifted uncertainly from one foot to the other.

Finally he sat down in an easy chair. "I–I've been praying for my mom and dad," he began. "I–I want to talk to them about trusting Christ as their Savior so they can go to heaven too."

"That's wonderful, Boyd," Kay told him. "Danny and Jim and I will be praying for them too."

"Thanks."

But there was something else bothering him. "I know they need Christ and I want to talk to them about Him, but Kay, I don't know how. I don't know what to say, and I–I don't know any Bible verses like Danny used when he talked to me the other night." He spoke seriously to her. "Would you help me to learn the verses I'd need to talk with someone about his soul?"

"Of course I would, Boyd. Why don't we go out here so we can sit at the table?" She gestured toward the kitchen.

They went to the kitchen and sat down, side by side, poring over the Bible. Jim Morgan was in his room studying, but he never did learn that Boyd Patterson had been there. It was after 9:30 p.m. when the new Christian finally got to his feet.

"I've got to get going, Kay. Thanks for helping me."

* * *

The next day Danny Orlis went back to Fairview on the bus to get Kay and Jim and the mission superintendent, Dr. Gordon. When they landed at the Cedarton airport that afternoon, a familiar couple got out of a car near the building and started toward them.

Danny turned to his young wife. "Do you recognize those people, Kay?" he asked her.

She squealed with delight. "Marilyn! Chuck!"

Danny leaped out of the plane and strode forward, holding out his big hand.

Kay, however, swept past him and enveloped Marilyn in her arms. "Marilyn!" she exclaimed. "It's so good to see you!"

They both cried a little.

"When we saw the plane circle town, we knew it must be you," the former Marilyn Forester explained, "so we decided to come out and get you."

"It's been so long since we've seen you," Kay responded. "I've been so anxious to see you, I could scarcely sleep at all last night."

Questions tumbled out, one upon the heels of another.

Finally Chuck Martin touched his wife's arm. "You two could stand out here and talk all night," he declared. "Why don't you at least let the rest of us get in where it's warm? I'm getting so cold now it'll take a week to thaw out."

Danny Orlis noticed that Marilyn Martin used her cane sparingly when she walked. Had he not known that she had been crippled by transverse myelitis, he might not even have noticed her limp. "I see Marilyn is getting around very well, Chuck," he remarked guardedly.

His old friend beamed. "God has been good. For a long time, we never thought she would ever be able to get rid of her crutches, but she did. She does all her own housework and helps at church in a way that makes a lot of people who are physically normal ashamed."

Kay and Marilyn were still talking excitedly as they reached the Forester home.

* * *

Carl and Mrs. Orlis were there that evening and so were Ron Orlis, Darlene Snyder, and John Porter. That night they all sat up talking until midnight. It was Harold Forester who finally suggested that they go to bed.

"We've got a big day tomorrow," he reminded them.

The following morning they were all up early and went out to the Bible Institute an hour before the all-day program was to begin.

Mary Orlis gasped when she saw that the parking lot was filled with cars. "Oh, Carl, look!" she exclaimed, her voice catching in her throat. "Everybody is here!"

He smiled and wiped his eyes unashamedly. "I was sitting here thinking the same thing," he agreed. "I've never seen anything like it in all my life."

Mrs. Forester turned to them. "There's never been anything here at CBI that has shaken the school the way Roxie's death and this missionary plane project have done. The Lord took hold of it in such a way that the young people didn't have to promote it very much. The money just seemed to come in without any effort on our part."

"When God is thoroughly behind something, it often goes in this way," Carl remarked quietly.

His wife, Mary, was eyeing the cars that jammed the parking lot. "My, but there are a lot of people here. And so early in the morning, too. I'm glad they are reserving seats for us."

Darlene was standing with Ron just inside the chapel door. They were looking out over the packed sanctuary.

"Ron," she half-whispered, "this is wonderful." Her voice broke as though she was about to cry.

"You can say that again," he told her. "They say this is the biggest crowd they've ever had for anything here at CBI and people are still coming." He reached down and squeezed her small fingers with his own big hand. "Thanks to you, Darlene."

She looked at him, her big eyes soft and luminous. "Don't thank me, Ron. Thank the Lord. He has blessed this whole affair in a very wonderful way. God is the one who has made this the success it is. We actually haven't done very much."

The day's program started with a special number

by the Cedarton Bible Institute Chorale followed by Scripture reading and prayer. Dr. Nielsen gave an opening address of welcome, and Dr. Gordon spoke briefly on the role youth have to play in forwarding the cause of Christ.

The program continued smoothly and with growing enthusiasm, but it remained for John Porter to bring the challenge of the day in his brief, halting speech accepting the plane. He wasn't a fluent speaker. In fact, he could scarcely have been called a speaker at all, but a hush fell over the vast crowd as he got to his feet.

"I want to thank each one of you for your part in helping provide the mission with this fine airplane," he began. "I don't have to tell you that it is badly needed or that I know God is going to use it for His glory."

He paused and something in his manner caused the listeners to lean forward expectantly.

"We have been hearing what wonderful things God has been working through His Spirit here at CBI and how so many of you young people have dedicated your lives to Him. But all of this has got me doing some serious thinking. I wonder how many of you people have been trying to give a few dollars for this plane when that isn't what God wants from you at all."

Someone in the crowd gasped.

"I mean it. Some of you gave money when God wants something far different from you. He may want some of you in His service."

The missionary took a deep breath and expelled the air with a rush.

"There are some hard places on the mission fields of the world today," he continued. "Indeed, as I talk with other missionaries and learn of the problems with which they are faced, I wonder if there are any harder places left in the world. There are hard places – places that take people with steel in their backbones and a love of Christ in their hearts great enough to cause them to seek to serve Him wherever they are called."

He looked from one to another, his eyes burning with a new fire.

"I didn't intend to say this today," he half-apologized. "I haven't even brought my message. But I want to know something as one person talking to another. How many of you who haven't dedicated your lives to God's service before are willing to come over here now and stand beside me?" He paused momentarily. "I'm asking you to make a public indication that you are willing to go or do whatever God directs, even to go to one of the *hard* places."

There was a moment's hesitation.

Then one young man stepped out, and then another, and another, until eight were standing beside the missionary.

CHAPTER 11

"NOT GRUDGINGLY, NOR OF NECESSITY"

Although the others had to leave early the next day to get back to their jobs and places of responsibility, Carl and Mary Orlis stayed with the Foresters for several days after the dedication of the plane.

The following afternoon Ron Orlis called his dad on the phone and insisted that the three of them go out to dinner that evening.

"That sounds like a fine idea, Ron," Carl agreed. "But don't you think we ought to ask Harold and Carrie Forester to go with us? After all, we've been staying with them almost a week."

"Not this time," Ron blurted. "We can go out to dinner with them tomorrow night or–or almost any other time you want to, but tonight I'd like to talk to you and Mom alone. I–I've got to talk to you."

"In that case we'll be glad to go," his dad answered.

Harold Forester loaned Carl and Mary Orlis his car and they drove out to Cedarton Bible Institute to pick up Ron shortly before six o'clock. He came out to the car hurriedly and got into the back seat.

"I'm sure glad you came alone," he told them. "I've just got to talk to you."

Mrs. Orlis turned and faced her son. "Now what is this all about, Ronald?" she asked, her eyes twinkling. "Do you have something you want to tell us about you and Darlene?"

Ron Orlis colored deeply. "Mom!"

"She's a lovely girl. I think it would be very nice if you got interested in her. You have our permission, doesn't he, Carl?"

She laughed, and only then did he realize that she was teasing him. He said no more until they were in the cafe and had given the waitress their orders. Then he leaned forward and lowered his voice.

"I suppose I could have talked in front of the Foresters. They're good friends of ours and–and I don't know that it would make any difference. But I got a bank draft a couple of days ago for more money than I've ever seen in my whole life. It just about floored me."

Carl Orlis nodded without surprise. "I knew that your father's estate was sizable."

"It's nice that you have it, Ron," Mary Orlis chimed in. "Now you won't have any more financial worries. You'll always have something to fall back on."

"I'm not going to keep it," he informed them quietly.

They stared at him as though their ears had deceived them.

"What?" Carl demanded.

"Money almost caused me to turn my back on God's plan for my life one time," Ron replied seriously. "I don't dare take any more chances, Dad."

Carl Orlis toyed with his glass of water for a brief moment. "That's a big decision you're making, Ron," he advised. "Once you do it you won't be able to undo it. You want to be very sure of what you want to do before you go ahead with it."

"I'm sure now." He spoke decisively. "I'm not going to keep it for myself."

Mary Orlis's eyes filled with tears. "Ron, that is a marvelous thing you are doing. I know Roxie would be so very happy."

"There's something else I plan on doing that Roxie would approve of," he went on. "Most of the money is going into the Lord's work, but I want to do something else with part of it. That's what I wanted to talk with you about tonight."

They waited patiently.

"You took Roxie and me in and gave us a wonderful Christian home," he spoke rapidly. "All that happened this week was the direct result of the teaching you gave us and the example you set for us. Roxie would have died outside the Lord if it hadn't been for you two and your prayers and the training you gave us."

Mary Orlis could contain herself no longer. Tears trickled unnoticed down her cheeks. "Don't say that, Ron," she managed. "We tried, but we failed so many times and in so many different ways."

"You can never make me believe that," he disagreed quietly.

The waitress came with their salads, and he waited until she was gone before continuing.

"You could have gotten paid for our care every month. But you wouldn't take any money – not even to pay back what you spent on us."

Carl Orlis spoke up. "You just shared what we had, Ron," he tried to explain. "The Lord provided. Besides, you will never know what a tremendous blessing you brought to our home. We couldn't take money for that."

"Maybe you didn't want to take it then, but now I want to do something about it. I want to do something to show you how much I appreciate what you did for Roxie and me."

They both stared at him.

"What do you mean?" his foster father asked.

"I want to turn part of this trust fund over to you."

Their eyes widened and for a short time they could not speak.

"You can't be serious!?"

"But I am. You've lived up on the Angle all your lives. With a little money you can build a small home down in Warroad and get a nice car and a few of the luxuries you've never had before."

Carl and Mary looked at one another and then back at him.

"But, Ron," he protested, "we have all that we need. We're comfortable and have a little money saved for emergencies. We don't need any more."

"But I want you to have it. You've both worked hard all your lives. You deserve to have things a lot easier than you have had in the past. With this money you can have it easier."

Mary Orlis laid her work-worn hand on his firm young arm, and when she spoke her voice broke with emotion. "You have no idea how this makes me feel – how it makes us feel, Ron," she answered. "Just knowing that you want to share what you have with us is a great thrill and one I'll never get over. But honestly, we don't need any more money than we have right now."

"Mom's right about this, Ron," Carl agreed. "You've made us very happy just letting us know that you think enough of us to–to want to do this for us. But we've got all we want – all we need."

Ron toyed with his fork. "I–I don't know what to say."

"What do you plan on doing with the money you are going to give to the Lord's work?" Carl asked.

"I'm going to buy floats for the plane first," he told them "and get some radio equipment and a few other things Danny said would be good to have. Then I'll give the rest of it for use in a worthy Christian radio ministry."

His eyes lighted. "You remember how we heard the program on the radio the last time we were over at Buckety Island on the Indian reservation and the chief said they listen to the program all the time? Roxie was going to spend her life bringing the gospel to the Indians. I think she would like to have it go for that purpose, don't you?"

"I'm sure of it," Carl answered.

Mary Orlis's eyes brightened. "Ron, you said you wanted to give some money to us, didn't you?"

"I certainly do, Mom, if you'll take it."

"Why don't you give it to the broadcast, too? You can give it in our names if you wish, as a memorial to Roxie."

"That's a wonderful idea!" Carl exclaimed.

"Are–are you sure that's what you want to do?"

"As sure as you are that you want to buy floats and give to the broadcast for the radio ministry yourself."

Ron saw the smile on their faces and broke into a broad smile himself. "Roxie would be so happy!" he exclaimed.

THE DANNY ORLIS SERIES

The Danny Orlis series, by Bernard Palmer, delivers a blend of adventure, mystery, and suspense through various settings—from the Canadian wilderness to Guatemalan jungles. Danny Orlis, an adept outdoorsman, skilled athlete, and committed Christian, employs his quick thinking, calm bravery, and biblical solutions to confront everyday problems and hair-raising dangers. Early stories focus on Danny navigating school life, sports, and outdoor challenges, while in later books, Danny and his wife Kay provide wisdom and guidance to youngsters facing lifelike situations and challenges. Having sold over two million copies, this series has made Palmer a renowned author in Christian youth literature. Palmer is also the author of the Felicia Cartright series and various other series for Christian youth.

AVAILABLE FROM WWW.ANEKOPRESS.COM